ONE MAN KNEW THE TRUTH
Paul Buher, head of the world's richest corporation, who raised the Son of Damien, and was enslaved by Him . . .

ONE WOMAN SUSPECTED THE TRUTH
Carol Wyatt, the daring, dedicated journalist who used her razor-keen mind and superbly seductive body to track evil to its secret lair . . .

ONE MAN FEARED THE TRUTH
Phillip Brennan, the American Ambassador to Britain, who did not want to believe that the world stood on the brink of satanic destruction, or that his own wife might be turned into a vessel of infernal lust . . .

But who could save humanity when the Boy grew strong enough to strip away his mask—to stand naked and tall in nightmare triumph . . . ?

OMEN IV
ARMAGEDDON 2000

The Best in Fiction From SIGNET

OMEN IV
ARMAGEDDON 2000

BY
GORDON McGILL

A SIGNET BOOK
NEW AMERICAN LIBRARY
TIMES MIRROR

PUBLISHER'S NOTE

This novel is a work of fiction. Names, characters, places, and
incidents are either the product of the author's imagination
or are used fictitiously, and any resemblance to actual persons,
living or dead, events, or locales is entirely coincidental.

SIGNET, SIGNET CLASSICS, MENTOR, PLUME, MERIDIAN AND NAL
BOOKS are published by The New American Library, Inc.,
1633 Broadway, New York, N.Y. 10019

First Printing, October, 1982

1 2 3 4 5 6 7 8 9

PRINTED IN THE UNITED STATES OF AMERICA

And when ye shall see Jerusalem compassed with armies, then know that the desolation thereof is nigh. . . .

For these be the days of vengeance, that all things which are written may be fulfilled.

LUKE 21:20, 22

Preface

For six weeks the disciples had stalked the woman. They watched her house while she slept, followed her to and from work, and waited for her when she visited friends. Since the death of their leader, their numbers had declined. Some had committed suicide. Others had given in to despair and would not move from their rooms, but those who survived were obsessed by revenge, and were the stronger for that.

On the day she visited the doctor's office, two disciples followed her and sat beside her in the waiting room. They took note of her strained expression. She was obviously in pain and they gloated over her discomfort.

"Miss Reynolds." The receptionist called to her and pointed toward a door. Slowly, with the gait of a cripple, she moved across the room and pushed the door open. A stranger looked up at her, a young doctor, fresh-faced and smiling. She blinked in confusion.

"Doctor Johnston has left the practice," he said. "Won't you sit down?"

She closed the door and sat by his desk.

"It's a sharp stabbing pain," she said, pressing her lower abdomen. "A sort of bloated feeling."

She coughed, brought up bile, and apologized. Gently the doctor led her to a couch and slowly examined her. When he had finished, he wrote a name and address on his prescription pad and handed it to her.

"This is a colleague of mine. Off Harley Street. He is a specialist in these matters. I want you to see him." He paused. "Soon."

She looked mutely at him for comfort.

"I'm sure it's nothing for you to worry about," he said.

As she got to her feet, she winced in pain. "Is there anything you can give . . . ?"

"I'm sorry," he said sharply. "I would rather not recommend painkillers at this stage."

He watched her leave and saw the two men look up, closed the door, and picked up the phone.

"Get me Chicago," he said.

As he waited for his connection, he smiled contentedly.

"In the midst of death there is life," he said to himself.

She lay facedown on the operating table, her arms held by two nurses. Her feet were tied into stirrups, forcing her legs apart. Her abdomen was bloated, the skin stretched and with the texture of a balloon. Her body convulsed rhythmically. She panted and looked imploringly at one of the nurses.

"It won't be long," said the nurse.

The pain zipped through her body and she opened her mouth, the scream almost choking her. The surgeon reached for a scalpel.

"I am going to make a small incision," he said. "It will help to relieve the pressure."

As he bent toward her, she screamed again and the nurse covered her face with a pad.

"No more chloroform," he snapped. "She needs to be conscious."

Her body convulsed.

"It is coming," said the surgeon. "Hold her."

Her back arched and she threw back her head to scream yet again, a howl of protest at the terrible thing that was happening to her. Then it was gone, out from inside her, and she flopped onto the table, shuddering like a fish on a slab. The surgeon handed something to a nurse, gazed for a moment at the floor as if in prayer, then moved to the door. He did not stop to wash his hands but walked slowly out into the corridor. A nurse followed him to the door and watched him approach an old couple who were sitting on a bench. She heard the familiar brutal words.

"We did everything we could."

The old woman sagged against her husband.

"The tumor was just too big," said the surgeon.

The nurse closed the door, turned, and took the bundle from her colleague. She gazed at it. It was a boy. Automatically she curtsied, then turned as she heard the slap of paws on the tiles. A large black dog, heavy-jawed, moved to her side. She laid the child on the floor and the dog bent over it, licking it clean.

The child's arms reached for it, the tiny fingers grasping at fur, and the nurse thought she could hear it chuckle. She glanced at the dead woman and motioned to one of the others to cover the body. Her face wrinkled in disgust, but when she looked down at the child, she smiled.

"It's an abomination," she said proudly.

In apartments and cottages, in offices and factories, the disciples murmured their approval. Those who had despaired were now alive with a new hope. And in a monastery in central Italy, a priest named De Carlo sat up in his narrow bed, his body damp with cold sweat, awakening from a nightmare in the sure and terrible knowledge that he had failed and that the worst was yet to come.

Part One

Chapter 1

The young man had been alone in one of the private lounges at Heathrow Airport for almost an hour, in which time he gazed at the runways and wandered to the bar, tempting himself to a drink and resisting the temptation. Every few minutes he checked his watch. Regularly he dipped into a pocket and gazed at a set of figures typed on a piece of paper. He had never met the old man but he knew that he needed to have every fact at his disposal because Paul Buher did not suffer fools gladly.

The loudspeaker chimed. A dingdong sound.

"Private charter Thorn Corporation from Chicago has just landed." The same dingdong accent.

The young man drew breath.

"Passenger Buher will arrive in the terminal lounge momentarily. Thank you."

He shot his cuffs and checked his tie. The chairman and majority stockholder of the Thorn Corporation was the most important and influential businessman in the Western world, which meant *the* world.

This was the man whose vision, some thirty years ago, had transformed an industrial giant of a company into what was now the biggest multinational complex on the globe. By a single masterstroke, Buher had realized that food was the most important economic item on the global shopping list and had turned Thorn into a vast fertilizer and soya manufacturer supplying the Third World.

The young man, many times, had impressed girls and younger executives with Buher's apocryphal statement, made all those years ago: "Our profitable future, lies in famine."

The man was a legend and something of a hero.

He was gazing out, looking for the Thorn jet, when the door opened and Buher stepped into the lounge, a tall man, straight-backed, strong-featured with tight white curly hair.

"Mr. Buher," the young man said. "My name is Harris. Welcome to London." He had not meant to sound like a tour guide, but the words simply tumbled out.

"Thank you, Harris," said Buher. "Nice of you to meet me."

Harris preened and hoped he wasn't blushing. "The car is at your disposal."

"Of course," said Buher. Obsequious little bastard, he thought.

In the limousine heading east along the M4, Harris snapped open the cocktail cabinet, but Buher shook his head.

"Any word from the Libyans?"

"None, sir," Harris said.

Buher nodded. "Okay. Extend their facility for three weeks and raise the interest rate a point and a half."

Harris blinked. "They might object, sir."

"They can object all they want. Wake me when we get to the office."

Buher closed his eyes and Harris wondered if he had just blundered.

The British head office of the Thorn Corporation had been built on the south bank of the Thames, constructed in the shape of a T, the Thorn logo, a smaller version of the headquarters building in Chicago. From his suite on the top floor, the chairman could look across the water at the City and the Bank of England. Turning to his left, he had a fine view of the Houses of Parliament. It was his habit, when phoning either place, to gaze directly toward it.

As soon as he reached his office, Buher asked for all incoming telexes of the last two days and ordered that he should not be disturbed for an hour. During that time, members of his staff began to congregate in the adjoining suite. They talked quietly, nodding a greeting at each newcomer. By the time the hour was up, the suite was filled with Thorn staff.

Buher's secretary checked her watch, knocked, and looked in.

"Happy birthday, sir," she said.

Buher looked up and smiled, then glanced past her at the others.

"Thank you," he said, stood, and motioned to them to come in.

They came at him in a recognized pecking order: first, the three vice-presidents, offering "Congratulations, Paul"; then the departmental heads, followed by company executives, whose faces were only vaguely familiar to him and who addressed him as "sir."

When everyone had shaken his hand, the group moved to one side to allow a young messenger boy to come forward. He carried a cake, baked in the shape of a T and sprouting candles. Silently the boy laid the cake on Buher's desk and backed off. Buher smiled, thanked him, and puffed at the candles. It took him three attempts and the effort made him lean back against his desk. The group cheered and a waiter appeared in the doorway, pushing a trolley.

"A little champagne?" asked his secretary.

"By all means," said Buher.

The waiter began popping corks. Buher took a glass and began accepting the congratulations of his staff.

"If I may say so Paul, you don't look anything like your age."

"You mean I'm wearing well?"

"No, I wouldn't exactly put it . . ."

". . . Are you celebrating tonight, sir?"

"No."

". . . Taking a break, Mr. Buher?"

"At this time?"

". . . I hope this year is as successful as the last, sir."

"More successful I would hope."

"Ah, yes, of course."

As he looked at them, he wondered who might turn out to be his successor. Not one of them seemed an obvious choice, neither here nor in Chicago. He had never been able to delegate and he recognized this as a weakness. What he needed was a forty-year-old Paul Buher.

"Well, here's to the big seven-oh."

He turned, to see Harris, his face flushed from the champagne, raising a glass to him.

Buher frowned.

"To the three score and ten." Harris grinned.

Buher shivered and stepped back. His secretary appeared at his elbow, smiling, showing a lot of teeth, taking Harris by the arm.

"What'd I say?" said Harris, looking confused.

"Get him out of here," said Buher softly.

The secretary led Harris toward the door, the others in turn backing away.

"What'd I do?" Harris voice squealed through the silence as Buher moved to his seat, slumped into it, and closed his eyes. When he opened them, only his secretary remained.

"I'm sorry, Mr. Buher . . ."

Buher shook his head. "It's okay."

"Is there anything I can get you?"

"Another thirty years," said Buher.

The woman smiled and left the room, wondering, as she closed the door, if Paul Buher might just be mortal, after all.

He was restless in his sleep, twitching and muttering. The woman raised herself onto her elbows and looked down at him. She traced a pattern on his chest, and his right hand fluttered. She grasped it and tickled his palm. Buher frowned and grunted something incomprehensible.

She smiled, took his fourth finger, and wiggled it. The finger closed around hers like a baby clutching at its mother. She could feel the rough skin of the birthmark on his finger, the squiggles that looked like numbers: three nines if you looked at them one way, three tiny sixes if seen from another angle, the tips meeting in a cloverleaf pattern. They seemed in her imagination to burn into her.

Buher twisted, his free arm thrashing as if he were swimming. His lips moved.

"What are you saying?" she whispered, leaning closer.

"Three score and ten," a faint murmur.

"Ssssh . . ." She held his hand tightly and he gripped her hand so that the birthmark scorched her. She yelped and tried to free her hand, but he held on.

"Paul," she squealed.

"Three score and ten," he rasped. "In the year of Armageddon. Seventy years."

She wrenched her hand free and rolled away from him. His lips continued to move, but there was no longer any sound. She glanced at her hand and saw that his birthmark had been burned into her finger like a brand. For a moment she lay mo-

12

tionless, staring at it, then put it to her lips and licked it, tracing the tiny sixes with the tip of her tongue, then turned, kissed Buher on the cheek, murmured a thank you, and fell into a deep, contented sleep.

Chapter 2

Over breakfast in his suite, Paul Buher carefully read through all the morning papers. They were unanimous in their praise of the Foreign Secretary's initiative in setting up a meeting between the Israelis and a group of Arab states. Peter Stevenson's political allies in Fleet Street wrote in superlatives about his statesmanship, some making wild predictions about a breakthrough and a possible solution to the Middle East problem. His opponents were less enthusiastic, but even they had to admit grudgingly that he had pulled off something of a coup.

Buher smiled. Such praise would help the man's ailing reputation and it was desirable that he should take some credit. Stevenson was a weak man, and weak men in positions of power suited Buher nicely.

He checked his watch and switched on the television set, tuning into the breakfast current-affairs program. The interviewer was filling in the background to the Foreign Office announcement of the meeting.

The Middle East, he said, had been in constant

14

turmoil ever since the foundation of the State of Israel in 1948, but never before had there been such a permanent condition of crisis. The jubilee bombings of Tel Aviv and Jerusalem had, for the past two years, kept the Middle East and, indeed the world, teetering on the brink of catastrophe.

Buher yawned and turned back to the papers until Stevenson was announced. The Foreign Secretary smiled at the camera. He was a High Tory with an angular patrician face which was a cartoonist's dream, and an inability to pronounce his r's, which was a gift to impersonators.

Buher listened carefully, checking that the man did not come out with anything unscripted. Stevenson talked of the difficulty in getting any dialogue since the 1998 attacks, but that now that he had succeeded in getting people around a table, he hoped that everyone would come to Lancaster House in a constructive frame of mind. Again Buher yawned.

"Go on," he murmured. "Tell them. You're just dying to tell them."

Only Buher knew the significance of the meetings that had been set up; only Buher, Stevenson, and the participants, only a handful of men, plus the Belgian whore who serviced the Foreign Secretary twice a month.

But Stevenson said only that he trusted no one would expect miracles from the meeting, but that, while the participants were talking to one another, their fingers were not poised on triggers. He smirked and nodded good morning to the camera.

"Pious bastard," said Buher.

He snapped off the set as his intercom buzzed.

"The ambassador for you, sir."

Buher grunted an acknowledgment and turned to the door as Philip Brennan, U.S. Ambassador to the Court of St. James, walked in, a tall man in his early forties, dark-complexioned and elegant with a crooked, boyish smile that charmed men and women and served him well in the corridors of diplomacy.

They shook hands, and Buher offered coffee, which Brennan accepted. The younger man nodded toward the television set.

"Did you see Stevenson? Did he say anything interesting?"

"Just the same tired old clichés," said Buher.

"Well, that's the problem. The Middle East is a cliché."

"What do you reckon?" Buher asked, squinting at him.

Brennan shrugged. "I suppose we'll read the entrails again. Trade Golan for the West Bank, swap Sinai for East Jerusalem. Keep our balls in the air—"

"And your entrails on the ground."

They grinned at each other and talked politics for twenty minutes, then Brennan glanced at his watch and said he had to be going. At the door, they again shook hands.

"Are you in town for long?" Brennan asked.

"No. Just a flying visit to check on the staff. I'll be back home Friday."

"Well, thanks for the coffee . . ."

16

"Philip," said Buher, still holding his hand, "I hear you're planning to run for the Senate."

Brennan smiled. "No one was supposed to know that."

"Look, I don't go in for unnecessary flattery, at least, only to keep fools happy, but I agree with those who predict a big career for you."

Brennan nodded, accepting the compliment.

"You could go all the way to the White House."

Again Brennan nodded. He was not going to deny the possibility.

"All I'll say for the moment is that any campaign needs funds." Buher paused. "And Thorn is not short of funds."

"That's nice to know, Paul, but isn't there a contradiction here? I am a Democrat, and the President, who you backed, is Republican."

"He is a weak man," said Buher. "It was hoped that he might grow in office."

"You haven't answered my question."

Buher smiled. "I didn't think it was a question."

Brennan opened the door and stepped out. "Thanks again for the coffee. I'll see you soon."

Buher watched him go and closed the door. Brennan was a strange mixture: a clever diplomat with no enemies, a man, thought Buher, who took integrity to the point of insanity. He might be a problem. It was just as well that precautions had been taken.

With that thought, he dismissed Brennan from his mind.

As the limousine eased its way west through the early-evening traffic toward the Oxford road, Buher stretched out in the back seat and gave in to the lethargy that was dragging at his eyelids. The night's sleep had not refreshed him. Normally, no matter what the pressure, he could recharge his batteries in three or four hours, but lately he tired easily. If it continued, he would see his doctor; meanwhile, he would not fight it. As he dozed, he thought of birthdays, the time when people took stock of their past lives and future ambitions. Buher had always been a tidy man. He liked the idea of being born in the middle month of a new decade. His father had slyly suggested that it had been planned that way.

He remembered the old man lecturing him: "By your twentieth birthday, June 1950, I will expect you to have begun to make your mark. By June 1970 you will have achieved much."

And indeed he had. His rise to the position of president of the Thorn Corporation had been spectacular. The plodders, men like old Bill Atherton, had expected him to overstretch himself, to fly too close to the sun and burn himself out, but he had survived while the others had been left behind.

Everything had gone according to plan until that dreadful day when Damien Thorn, the last of the Thorn dynasty, had been betrayed and murdered. It had been eighteen years but still the anger festered in him.

He grunted to himself and opened his eyes, to

see the driver glancing curiously at him in the rearview mirror. Buher took a bottle of vitamin pills from his pocket and chewed a handful. His stomach was churning with the tension of seeing the boy again. He would be seventeen now, at that age when adolescents began to show the first signs of maturing toward adulthood. He wondered what signs the boy would show. The disciples said he had grown a couple of inches and put on weight.

Buher belched. It would be his stomach that killed him. He recalled the words of his doctor— something about stress. Everyone, the man had said, had a target organ that self-destructed. Some had headaches; others found their blood congealing, putting the heart under strain. With Buher, it was the stomach, but only the boy had the power to induce such tension. No politician, no business opponent, no President of the United States, had such an effect on him—only the boy.

He glanced through the window as the limousine turned off the motorway toward the narrow country road that led to Pereford. The driver eased the big machine around sharp bends and along a road flanked with high hedges. Rabbits darted into the hedges and the windshield was a mess of kamikaze insects.

"Here we are, sir." The driver's voice crackled through the intercom as the car pulled up outside the gates. Since Damien's death, a security system had been installed, the large wrought-iron gates by the lodge being electronically operated. The driver touched a switch on the dashboard and the gates opened. Half a mile up the drive, Buher could see the west wing of the great mansion. There would be the best brandy, logs would be burning in the drawing room. Soon he could relax.

The limousine crunched gravel and stopped. George, the butler, was standing by the doorway; he ushered Buher inside and reached for his case, wheezing that it was good to see him.

Buher went straight to the drawing room, poured himself a brandy, and gazed around the room.

The house was a masterpiece of understated extravagance. He ran his fingers along the oak paneling and stroked the heavy velvet drapes, then looked up at the portraits. Robert Thorn; his brother, Richard; his son, Damien. He shivered and moved to the fireplace. Although it was high summer, a log fire burned furiously. He stood with his back to it, warming his hands, waiting.

The butler looked in.

"Dinner will be ready in twenty minutes, sir."

Buher nodded. "How is he?"

"He is well, sir."

"Can I see him?"

"If you can find him, sir."

Buher nodded and left the room, taking his drink with him. He crossed the hall and climbed the curved staircase to the first landing and made his way along a gallery to a darkened corridor leading to the west wing of the house. He could feel his heart thump and his stomach churn as he reached the boy's bedroom. Gently he tapped on the door and listened. There was no sound. He knocked again, then pushed the door open and stepped inside.

The room was empty except for a narrow bed; the walls and ceiling were painted maroon. Buher blinked, reached for the light switch, and snapped it on. Nothing; there was no light bulb in the room. He moved to the bed and gazed at a collage of newspaper photographs, flanked by two large framed pictures. The one on the right was a portrait of Damien Thorn, just the head and shoulders. The other was a grave and a headstone. Buher peered at the words chiseled in granite, half-obscured by weeds:

KATHLEEN REYNOLDS
BELOVED DAUGHTER
1949–1982

He sniffed and knelt on the bed, peering at the collage. There was a shot of Warsaw Jews being forced from the ghetto at gunpoint toward the trucks, waiting to take them to Auschwitz. There was another of mass graves; there were portraits of Hitler and Idi Amin, Mussolini's posturing jaw, Stalin's leer. Harry Truman smiled through a mushroom cloud above the devastation of Hiroshima. Churchill puffed cigar smoke over a charred signpost saying Dresden; Henry Kissinger smiled as he received the Nobel Peace Prize, while Pol Pot stood at his elbow, his feet straddling a mass grave of skulls and twisted bones.

Splashed across the collage was one word, red-painted in a childish hand:

REHEARSALS

Buher blew bad air from his lungs, took a gulp of brandy, and left the room, glad to be gone.

He walked deeper into the west wing, along a second corridor, and smelled the dog before he saw it. He approached it slowly, peering at the yellow eyes that gazed back at him from the depths of the corridor. It raised its massive black head, slowly got to its feet, and padded toward him, an enormous animal, heavy-jawed, the power concentrated in its neck and shoulders. Its breath was foul. It stopped and looked at Buher, the head level with his stomach. For a moment, man and dog stared at each other, the dog sniffing, its head bobbing as it worked out the scent; then it grunted and moved to one side, a sentry giving permission to pass.

Buher crept past to the black door at the end of the corridor, raised his hand to knock, thought better of it, and pushed the door open.

The room was circular, painted black, the roof supported by six columns. It was windowless, lit by a single black candle mounted on a plinth.

The fluttering light illuminated a life-size wooden effigy of Christ, nailed face-on to a cross, the chest pressed against the upright, the legs wrapped around it, a nail piercing the feet, the arms stretched along the beam and nailed through the backs of the hands.

The figure was naked. A dagger protruded from the spine, driven in to the hilt, which itself was engraved in the shape of Christ on the cross.

Six feet from the cross stood the embalmed body of a man. It too was naked and appeared to stand unsupported. The arms were stretched out, palms facing outward. The candlelight flickered in the eyes, making them seem alive. The mouth was twisted in a sardonic grin as the corpse gazed directly into the agonized face of the Christ figure.

A boy wearing a black cassock knelt at the feet of the corpse, his arms raised, grasping the dead hands, gripping them so that his knuckles showed white.

Buher, straining, could hear his low monotone.

"Father, give me strength and let your spirit grow in me. Father give me strength . . ."

The litany was repeated without pause, a murmur without inflection, the boy hardly seeming to draw breath. Buher gazed at him, then looked up into the dead face of Damien Thorn. Slowly and instinctively he made a reverse sign of the cross, backed out of the room, and silently closed the door.

The dog watched him, listening until the sound of his footsteps died away, then it lay once more on guard, ears back, picking up the hum of the boy's voice.

Buher waited for him in the dining room. He sipped brandy and gazed blankly at the television, seeing nothing, and when he looked up, the boy was standing in the doorway. He had changed into a shirt and jeans, and he had grown, as the disciples had said. He was now almost as tall as his father had been, and the resemblance was remarkable.

"You look tired," the boy said, and Buher noticed that his voice had deepened.

"It's nothing," said Buher. "Nothing but old age."

"Perhaps you should give up sex."

Buher smiled. "In the old days, it was stimulating. Now I simply become lethargic."

The boy sat down as George came in with the dinner trolley.

"You have a report for me," the boy asked, ignoring the butler.

Buher nodded, reached into his pocket, and flipped over a memo. The boy read through it without blinking, then looked up sharply.

"The Libyans won't default, will they?"

Buher shook his head. "We have their tails in a crack. There's nowhere else they can go."

The boy nodded, folded the memo, and handed it back.

"Good. So everything's on course?"

Buher frowned. It was a strange phrase.

"Everything is fine?" the boy said, correcting himself with a smile.

"The British are trying to organize their own little Camp David over Jerusalem, but they cannot succeed."

"Good," said the boy, tucking a napkin into his shirt. He turned, thanked the butler, and began to eat.

During the meal there was no small talk. The boy ate hungrily, gulped his wine, and between mouthfuls interrogated Buher.

"I heard that Simon was in trouble at the Knesset. . . .

"How is Bradley coping at the White House?

"When will the Zimbabwe coup take place?"

Buher answered him patiently. He had forgotten how bright the boy was, how quickly his mind grasped and stored details. He was so like his father, lacking only the charm of Damien Thorn, but that would come in time.

They were sipping coffee when the butler appeared with a note, which he handed to Buher, then turned to the boy.

"I'm afraid it's the woman again, sir."

The boy yawned as Buher glanced at the note.

"She says she was a midwife to you," said Buher.

George shrugged. "She has been turning up at the lodge for over a week now, sir. A bit of a nuisance."

Buher glanced at the boy. "She wants a last blessing from you."

Again the boy yawned.

Buher crumpled the note into a ball and flicked it toward the fire. "Send her in," he said. "But make sure that she is who she says she is."

"Yes, sir."

The butler left and the boy looked back at Buher.

"You are sure about Bradley?"

Buher sighed. The boy was obsessive and persistent. There seemed to be nothing in his mind except business. There were no outside interests, nothing that would have distracted other young men; but then, he was not like other young men.

Again the door opened and they turned, to stare into the wrinkled face of an old woman. She sat hunched in a wheelchair, a rug around her legs, a shawl over her shoulders. Her hands were twisted, the fingers seemingly glued together. The rug and the shawl were heavy, but they could not disguise her frailty. Buher reckoned that she could not weigh more than eighty pounds. She touched a button on the chair and it moved toward them, the motor hissing, the rubber tires squeaking. She stopped at the table, her eyes fixed on the boy, reached for two crutches fixed to the chair, and slowly raised herself to her feet. Buher got up to help her, but she shook her head at him.

"I'll manage," she said in a voice that squeaked like the tires. Her bones crackled as she moved, and when she was fully upright, her face was at a level with the boy's.

"My name is Mary Lamont," she said. "As a nurse, I was present at your birth."

The boy said nothing.

"The very evening you were born, the arthritis began in my hands. I have been in pain ever since. I take drugs, but they make me ill. When I dream, I believe that God is punishing me."

"He would," said the boy.

"I can no longer stand the pain, and so I will shortly take my life. But before I die, I wanted to see you. I wanted to see what I had helped bring into the world."

The boy spread his hands wide and offered his profile. "I hope you are pleased," he said.

The woman shrugged and her bones creaked.

"Will you give me your blessing?"

The boy nodded, got to his feet, and looked down at the emaciated figure before him. He laid his hands on her forehead and she closed her eyes, then shuddered and looked up at him.

"I have always tried to serve. I helped at your birth and I killed a baby for your father."

The boy's hands tightened on her head and his expression hardened into a scowl.

"I was there when your father asked us to slay the children born on the day that the Son of God was reborn. I did my duty and I always hoped that—"

"You hoped what?" His voice was clipped and precise as he glared down at her.

"I hoped that I might have been the one to eliminate the Christ child."

"Then your hopes can die with you," he snarled, and stepped back from her, wiping his hands on his shirt as if they were contaminated. "You failed him. You all failed him. The Son of God still lives. Every day I am aware of his benign, stultifying influence. His power increases every hour. He is everywhere, waiting for me." He stepped back, and when he spoke, the saliva sprayed the face of the old woman. "You failed my father, and you failed me."

The woman sobbed quietly, the tears dribbling down the deep creases in her face and running into the corners of her mouth. She raised one twisted hand to wipe them away as the boy stepped forward and glared at her.

"You think that your pain is the work of God," he said, shaking his head. "No. He punishes humanity for what He considers to be its sins. My father does not punish. He never punishes, except for failure. That he cannot condone."

The woman looked at him beseechingly. "But I did all I was asked. I could do no more. What else . . . ?"

The boy turned away. "Get your bones out of my sight."

She stepped back and sank into the wheelchair. The tears were running unchecked now.

"Please forgive me," she said softly.

"You failed him." He turned his back on her. "May your spirit sink forever in the dead sea of sanctimony."

A sob broke from her and Buher moved toward the chair.

"Leave her," said the boy. "Let her go."

Buher stopped, wanting to comfort the woman but unable to resist the boy's power. Slowly she turned the wheelchair and trundled out of the room; for a moment Buher could hear the squeak of the tires on the tiles and the rhythmical sobbing. Then the door was closed behind her and there was silence.

Buher turned to the boy.

"Don't you think . . . ?"

But the boy ignored him and pushed past him, out of the room, taking his terrible anger with him.

Chapter 3

By the time she had reached the taxi waiting for her at the gate, she had managed to dry her tears. She smiled at the driver and made small talk all the way to the home, where she went straight to her rooms, guiding the wheelchair through the living room to her bedroom, where no one had ever been permitted entry.

It was painted black. Two photographs hung on the wall, one of Damien Thorn, the other of a young woman. The only furniture was a bed and a writing desk and chair. There were two bookshelves, one filled with biblical interpretation texts, the other with pornography. She moved to the shelves and touched the books, then reached for a paperweight on her desk and threw it at the photograph of Thorn. But she had no strength. It thudded harmlessly on the floor and she panted with the exertion. Slowly she levered herself out of the chair, took the other photograph from the wall, hobbled to her bed, moving like a wounded insect, and stretched out, gazing at the portrait. Her father had taken it just a few months before she left home. She had been, she realized, a classic case—lonely, timid, and naive—until she met the crazy boy who had nicknamed himself Belial ... After that, it was chaos.

At first she had resisted the temptations, but once she had begun, she took to it with the zeal of the convert. The group accepted her because, as a nurse, she had access to the most exotic drugs. The chaos had lasted for months, night and day indistinguishable, and then one morning she had awakened from what she thought was a nightmare but turned out to be real. They had made her fornicate with a dog, and when she awoke and rubbed the dried saliva from the back of her neck, she found a scar—three tiny sixes in a cloverleaf pattern—and scrawled on the wall above her bed, the words from Revelation:

Let he who hath understanding
Reckon the number of the Beast:
For it is a human number,
Its number is Six Hundred and Sixty-six.

She had gone, in a panic, back to her parents and begged forgiveness, telling them only a little of what had happened; but they, in their righteousness, turned their backs on her, and so, before she left, she told them the rest. When she got back to Belial and the others, she was made welcome, then told what she had become.

She closed her eyes and sighed, thinking of Damien Thorn's instructions and how she had killed the child, a newborn baby in an incubator. It had been so simple. She had turned off the oxygen for a moment. She remembered its name: Michael Thomas, a tiny thing in intensive care who was just beginning to put on weight, before she turned off his oxygen.

She sighed and closed her eyes . . .

The little man with the dog collar smelled of peppermint and he leaned toward her, smiling, showing bad teeth. She looked down and saw his fingers scrabbling with the matchbox, pulling out a match and lighting it with a flick of his thumbnail. She was young, little more than a child, in the first swellings of puberty, and she watched him come closer, trusting him as her parents had instructed, obeying him as God's messenger. The light of the match blinded her and she closed her eyes, smelling the peppermint, his lips at her ear: "Just a taste of what will happen if you are sinful . . ."

She screamed as the flame was pressed against her hand.

"Do not stray from the ways of God or your soul will burn . . ."

She screamed again and opened her eyes. The priest's face leered at her, his lips fluttering at her cheek, one hand on her breast.

"An eternity of agony. The flesh that burns but is not consumed . . ."

She felt the grubby hands stroking her and yet again she screamed and closed her eyes, and when she opened them, a young man stood before her and she knew that he was Michael Thomas, a handsome boy, smiling forgiveness at her and with him another whose face was indistinct, moving

toward her, holding her burned hand and soothing it, his voice telling her to trust in God, that
there was still room for her in his father's kingdom....

She awoke and gazed at the photograph of Damien Thorn, but instead there was a young face,
still indistinct, his words echoing from her dream:
"Repent. There is always time."

She pushed herself off the bed and hobbled
toward the desk, reached for a pen and a writing
pad. She wrote slowly, the pen gripped in her fist,
almost upright, the very motion of writing causing
her to wince in pain.

"Forgive me, Father, for I have sinned . . ."

She wrote without pausing for two hours, the
pen slowly moving across the pages as if it had a
life of its own. When she had finished, she reached
for an envelope and an address book.

"Father De Carlo," she wrote. "Monastery of
San Benedetto, Subiaco, Italy."

There was no other to whom she could confess
or offer repentance. He was the only one who
would understand, the only one who would believe. She looked up. It was dawn. She reached for
the phone and called a taxi.

On the journey east, back toward the memories
of her childhood, she wondered if De Carlo would
forgive her. Maybe he would think that her repentance was no more than a last-minute act of
desperation, an insurance policy against eternal
hell-fire. She clutched the letter in her shawl and
felt the tears run again, crying for herself, for her

wasted blasphemous life, and then for the baby she had killed. Finally she cried for the abomination whose birth she had witnessed.

"Here we are," said the driver, his voice jolting her back into the present. She gazed up at an office building where the convent had been, then sighed, but at least there was a mailbox.

"I'll post it for you, love," said the driver, but she was struggling out on her crutches. "Suit yourself, then," he said, and waited until she had got back in.

"It's done," she said. "Take the second on the left, please."

The church was still standing, but it was a ruin, just a shell with no roof and a battered sign saying ST. LUKE's and covered in graffiti, the place where she had been christened and her father and grandfather before her.

Again she levered herself out of the cab and stood on the pavement, which trembled to the concussion of nearby jackhammers. A builder's sign with the word "demolition" had been fixed to the steeple, and the churchyard was roped off.

"Is nothing sacred?" she whispered as she made her way toward the church door. She ducked under the rope and her bones crackled. She turned back briefly. The taxi driver had slumped back in his cab, his eyes closed, dozing while he waited for her.

Slowly she made her way up the path. The great oak door was gone. She stepped inside and gazed through the shattered roof, covering her ears to muffle the sound of the demolition hammers. The whole place seemed to shudder and she could feel the flagstones vibrate through her shoes. The pews had been torn out and only the altar and pulpit remained. Slowly she stumbled up the nave and looked up through the shattered roof, her eyes smarting from the dust. She blinked and gazed into the face of Christ, the great stone statue she remembered from her childhood, standing on a plinth next to the pulpit.

The face of Christ was serene, bearded, the gaze directed across the nave of the church toward a nonexistent congregation, the hands held together in prayer across the chest. She knelt before it, bowed, and began to pray, half-remembered words, praying in silence; then she recalled a psalm, raised her head, and began to sing.

The jackhammers seemed to join in, beating out a rhythm; the statue swayed, the face of Christ obscured by a rising and thickening cloud of dust.

She struggled to her feet and touched her neck. The scab had gone. The skin was smooth. She sobbed again, but this time with tears of joy.

"I am redeemed," she whispered.

The wall behind her crumbled with the force of the hammers and the statue rocked on the plinth. She drew herself erect and raised her arms toward it.

"Welcome me, Lord, into Thy kingdom."

Her last sight was the face of Christ toppling toward her. The pointed beard pierced her skull, the stone fingers speared into her emaciated chest. And her last scream was one of exultation.

A demolition worker found her moments later. He thought he had heard a scream and climbed over the wall to investigate, saw her beneath the statue, her arms and legs clasped around the body as if in the act of copulation, one leg twitching in a final death spasm, her eyes filled with blood, staring at him over the shoulder of Christ. And in the instant before he fainted, he thought he saw her smile at him.

Chapter 4

In his hotel in Rome, Philip Brennan was wakened by a call from his secretary. He gently pushed his wife off him and reached for the receiver, grunted good morning, and yawned.

"Any overnight alterations to the agenda? . . . Okay, so send up the dispatches with the coffee and I'll be down in half an hour."

He replaced the receiver and slipped from the bed. Margaret did not move. Last night had been exhausting; lately, lovemaking had become a brutal business. She had come to enjoy it that way recently and it excited him, but sometimes he wished that it was more gentle and affectionate. He winced in the shower as the spray hit the new scratches on his back, and as he soaped himself, he was aware of the teeth marks on the fleshy part of his chest. Rome was supposed to be a romantic city, he thought, but all it had done was make Margaret more ravenous.

By the time he had dressed, the overnight package was waiting for him. He sipped his coffee and checked the latest intelligence reports from Tel Aviv against the overnight wire copy describing troop movements in the Golan Heights. It was like a playback of every news bulletin he had heard since he was a child. Little had changed. The same words were spoken, the same place-names, either being bombarded or doing the bombarding. The only change recently was in the intensity. Since the jubilee attacks, there was more tension, and since the Libyans had the bomb, more fear.

He was glad that he was merely an observer on this Roman trip: two days of watching, listening, and making contacts. The press had picked up on his visit and suggested he was being groomed for something bigger than ambassadorial material. Questions about his future were adroitly fielded by the press attaché while he, in turn, had given an honest "no comment" to speculation. He did not know what was being planned for him, but he knew what plans he had for himself.

His coffee finished, he kissed his wife and left the room, feeling good and ready for a new day.

Late that afternoon, the main parties involved in the talks issued a joint communiqué about fruitful discussions taking place in a constructive atmosphere. The seasoned commentators read through the two-page statement, searching for nuances, and came to their own joint conclusion that nothing had been achieved. The classic blockage had still to be shifted and there was no sign of the warring parties coming face to face over a table. The young men of the PLO were veterans of campaigns in Syria and Lebanon, to whom the word "compromise" was an obscenity, while the Knesset, since the bombings, had become even less amenable to pressure or advice from outside.

It was, as always, a stalemate; and Brennan, listening to the speeches in the debating room and the talk in committee rooms, began to wonder if he would be good enough for the position of Secretary of State. Each route toward a solution came to a dead end. Whenever someone came up with a suggestion, there was another who would abort it before it had reached even discussion phase.

The meeting over, he crossed the foyer, deep in thought. At first he did not hear his name being called, and turned sharply as someone tugged at his sleeve. A small burly man looked up at him. He was carrying a velvet pouch.

"Signor Brennan, my name is Facchetti, hotel security."

Brennan nodded a greeting.

"I am sorry to disturb you, sir, but we have a man in our office who wants to see you."

"Would you refer him to my—"

"He says he is a monk, sir," said Facchetti. "But he is a very worldly monk." He handed Brennan the pouch. "He was carrying this."

Brennan took it and drew out a dagger. He caught his breath as he gazed at it, a vicious weapon, the blade triangular, the hilt worked in the shape of a crucifix with a Christ figure wrapped around it.

"He asked at the front desk for hotel security," said Facchetti. "When one of my men saw him, he said that he wanted to see you. He then handed

my man the dagger. He said that if he had request-
ed an appointment and the dagger was found on
him, then wrong conclusions would have been
drawn."

"Quite," said Brennan. He touched the blade
and yelped as it drew a sliver of blood.

"He has something to say to you about the dagger. Normally we would not have bothered you,
but—"

Brennan held the dagger and gazed into the agonized face of the Christ, touched the twisted
body. Despite his better judgment, he was intrigued.

"Send him up, would you?" he said. "I'll see
him briefly, but you hold on to the knife, okay?"

He handed the dagger to Facchetti and made
his way to the elevators. On his way up to his
suite he rubbed his hands together. They were
clammy. He shivered slightly. From childhood he
had had a fear of knives. The thought of the steel
piercing skin and slicing through flesh made him
feel ill. The pain must be unimaginable. As for
crucifixion . . . Again he shivered, and not for
the first time, he wondered about the sort of religion that was forever depicting its leader and
inspirational force in such terrible agony. It was
no wonder that some of Christ's followers were
odd. To him religion was a convention, a once-a-
week exercise. He had never looked deeply into it.
Somehow, in the year 2000 it seemed a bit irrelevant.

Margaret had left a note saying she would be
back in time for dinner. There were some telex

messages on his desk. As he read them, there was a knock on the door. He opened it, to see Facchetti with a young man wearing a brown cassock and sandals. The face was boyish and handsome, but the expression was strained and anxious, the look of an older man, the fatigue and despair seeming out of place.

He stood back to let him enter, then held up his hand to Facchetti, who backed off with the worried shrug of a man whose job is to protect other men.

"I'll be okay," Brennan said, and nodded to him.

The monk tried a smile. "My name is Brother Francis," he said in clear English. "From Subiaco. It is good of you to see me."

"I don't have long," said Brennan, gesturing toward a chair.

"What I have to say, you will find hard to believe," said the monk. "Indeed, I do not expect you to take my word." He paused. "How long are you in Rome, Mr. Brennan?"

"I'm leaving tomorrow."

The monk sighed. "I am asking you to postpone your departure for a few hours and come with me. I have been sent by a priest named Father De Carlo. You may have heard of him?" The last sentence was a plea.

"No. I can't say that I—"

"Father De Carlo cannot travel. He is old and frail. If I say to you that you must help him because the future of mankind depends on it, then you will think I am being—what is the word?"

41

"Melodramatic?"

"Yes, and if I tell you why, then you will think I am insane. All I ask is that you read the letter. You will think it is the ravings of a madwoman, but it is not."

Brennan, again despite his better judgment, was impressed by the monk. By describing himself in such a way he had disarmed criticism.

"Are you a religious man, Mr. Brennan?"

"Only on Sundays, I'm afraid," he said, wondering why he was apologizing.

"You are Protestant?"

"Yes."

"Let me quote you something." He held his hands together as if in prayer. " 'When ye shall see Jerusalem compassed with armies, then know that the desolation thereof is nigh. . . . For these be the days of vengeance, that all things which are written may be fulfilled.' I quote from Saint Luke."

Brennan again glanced at his watch. "Yes, well, I'm afraid . . ." He had heard enough. He felt like he did when the Jehovah's Witnesses came to the door. At first you were polite, but eventually their persistence caused you to be rude.

The monk stood up with him and backed off toward the door. "Hear these words, which you will think insane. Father De Carlo came to England eighteen years ago. He witnessed the second coming of Christ. He destroyed the physical body of the son of Satan."

Brennan smiled wearily and took the young man by the arm, leading him toward the door.

"But the spirit of the Antichrist lives on, Mr. Brennan. Only the daggers can destroy it."

Brennan opened the door.

"All I ask is that you read the letter. Please suspend your skepticism. I will telephone you tomorrow."

"Facchetti," Brennan shouted, pulling the door open. The little man bounced forward, grabbed the monk by his hood, and dragged him out of the room.

"Good-bye, Brother Francis," Brennan said.

"The spawn of the devil still lives, Mr. Brennan. It must be destroyed."

Brennan grinned and closed the door, and as the lock clicked into place, he heard the voice of the monk fading into the distance.

"Suspend your disbelief in the name of God . . ."

An hour later, having made his calls, Brennan slumped in the chair and picked up the envelope. Yawning, he slit it with his thumb and drew out six sheets of photocopy, wrinkling his nose at the whiff of copying fluid, a smell that always brought to his mind a picture of embalmed corpses. There was a note with the letter:

"What this woman says is true, God help us. Please come."

It was signed: "Father De Carlo, Subiaco."

He spread the letter on the desk and smiled. He had come across such writing before, the double-fisted style, one of his aides had called it, the style of UFO spotters and conspiracy theorists who wrote to him when he was still a small fry in the diplomatic service. Now such letters were screened by his staff.

"Forgive me, Father, for I have sinned . . ."

He read the first page, then shook his head and reached for the Scotch bottle.

"Jesus Christ Almighty," he said, and began to laugh.

The Brennans had accepted a dinner invitation that night from a British journalist, one of Fleet Street's senior diplomatic correspondents. James Richard was tall and elegant, his accent impeccably BBC, and he had never been seen without a carnation in his buttonhole. He had many rules of behavior, the most important being that off-the-record conversations should be exactly that. By maintaining such discretion he had become trusted by politicians and disliked by the colleagues on the paper that paid his salary.

They dined in the hotel restaurant, Margaret turning heads as she made her way to the table, tall, auburn-haired, wearing a simple black dress. Brennan was proud of her. She knew exactly how to behave. He knew that she would charm Richard but would not flirt with him. Once, in their privacy, she had said that it would not do for a future First Lady to be anything other than perfectly behaved. He had laughed for a moment until he realized she was serious.

The talk ranged from the meeting to gossip, from sport to anecdote. Richard did most of the talking, weaving stories out of seemingly trivial incidents. He was a born raconteur and the Brennans were content to listen.

It was not until they had reached the brandy that Richard leaned back and put the question.

"I hear that you received a visitation today," he said with mock pomposity. "From the clergy."

Brennan nodded. It did not surprise him that Richard knew about the monk. He seemed to know about things before they happened.

"A young man from a monastery somewhere," he said. "A trifle deranged."

He went on to describe the dagger, and as he did so, he felt the perspiration run down his arms.

"And what did he want, this mad monk?" Richard asked.

Brennan shrugged. "I won't bore you with details. But how about this? The spawn of the devil is alive and well and living in England."

"My God," Richard said, throwing back his head and laughing.

"Some old woman wrote the monastery with a story I won't repeat over dinner."

"Oh, go on," said Richard. "Maybe I can pass it on to the *National Enquirer*."

"You wouldn't," Margaret said.

Richard smiled at her. "Of course not. All this is off the record. Even devil spawn is off the record."

The waiter appeared with coffee.

"I think," said Margaret, "we should change the subject."

And they did.

An hour later, in bed, Margaret Brennan turned to her husband.

"What was the story you couldn't repeat over dinner?"

"Obscene," he said, yawning.

"Tell me."

There was an urgency in her voice, a tone he recognized. At first in their marriage he had been the one to invent erotic fantasies for them to play out, but lately she had been the instigator, and the extent of her imagination amazed him.

"Go on," she said. "Tell me."

He was tempted to tell her that he needed a good night's sleep, that he was exhausted, but he fought the lethargy. Christ, he thought, I'll be complaining about headaches next.

"It's disgusting," he said as she snuggled against him. "According to this woman, one of my predecessors, Damien Thorn, screwed some English girl. From the BBC, would you believe?"

"And?"

"And a few months later, after Thorn had died of a heart attack, probably induced by the aforementioned activity, she gave birth"—he chuckled, wondering how to phrase it—"and not by way of the womb."

He expected her to either laugh or grimace, but there was only silence. Then she whispered, "Damien Thorn was the most handsome man I have ever seen."

He glanced at her. "You met him? I didn't know."

"I just saw his picture. When I was a schoolgirl, I had dreams about him."

Again there was silence, and then she turned on her side, her back to him.

"What was the woman's name?"

"Kate," he said. "Kate somebody."

"Kate," she whispered. "Kathleen, Cathy, Katerine," her voice was no more than a whisper now, the accent changing until it was that of an Englishwoman. "Kate," she whispered, "call me Kate."

He turned to her, knowing what she wanted.

"What's your name?" he whispered.

"Kate," she said again, pressing her elbow into the pillow and raising herself.

As they made love, he saw their bodies reflected in the window. Through the glass, the night sky was cloudless and the stars were studded into their reflections.

It was perverse and he reveled in it, at the sound of her voice in a strange accent, urging him to do unspeakable things to her, calling him Damien, crying out in pain as he penetrated her body; and as he glanced over her shoulder at the window, he was aware of some trick of the light: flickering among the white pricks of starlight, her eyes gleamed back at him with a dull yellow glow.

The next morning, one of the hotel front-desk clerks looked up from behind the counter into the anxious face of a young man dressed in a cassock.

"My name is Brother Francis . . ." he began.

"Ah, yes," said the clerk. "There is a package

for you." He reached below the counter and handed over the pouch and an envelope. The envelope had been resealed with tape. The monk opened it, looked inside, and sighed.

"May I speak to Mr. Brennan please, suite three four—"

"He has checked out, I'm afraid, sir."

"Did he leave me any message?"

"I'm afraid not, sir. Just what you have in your hand."

The monk closed his eyes and fought back the tears, wondering how he was going to tell his priest that he had failed.

Chapter 5

It took James Richard only three days to tell the story of Brennan and the monk to one of the executives on the paper. They were having an early-morning drink—a heart-starter, as Richard called it—and as they laughed at the absurdity of it, the description of the dagger stirred something in the recesses of the other man's brain. Back at the office, he called out to a young woman reporter and crooked a finger at her to follow him into his office.

Carol Wyatt was twenty-two and had been in Fleet Street for only two months. Already she had begun to make a name for herself. She was a natural beauty, small and slender, with delicate features, long-necked, with unusually large brown eyes, the left one slightly off-center so that she looked perpetually bewildered and vulnerable. Slim-legged, she was pretty enough to attract lecherous advances from some of the men and bitchy comments from the women, but even the bitchiest were forced to admit that she was a valuable addition to the staff.

She had shown her bosses that her vulnerable

expression concealed a sharp brain and an ambitious nature, and she was marked down as promising; her one mistake had been to mention in a bar that her schoolgirl nickname was Bambi. The name stuck.

"Yes, Bill," she said, smiling as she closed the door behind her.

"It's summer," said the executive.

"Correct."

"Which means that we need to stockpile some features for the slow days."

With an effort Carol kept her smile intact.

"I've just been talking to tricky Dicky and he reminded me of a tale—"

"Unusual for a start," she said.

"Fifteen, twenty years ago," he continued. "A series of corpses, all involving nasty religious daggers. Our friends at the Yard were baffled. Check it out from cuts, will you? I think they were called the Crucifixion Killings, something like that. About eight hundred words. We'll use it in the Unsolved Crime spot."

"You're not doing that again, are you?" she said. It wasn't much in the way of rebellion, simply a mild protest.

He ignored her, spun around on his seat to check a page proof. She was dismissed.

On her way to the library she grumbled aloud to herself. "Bloody cuttings job. Thought this was supposed to be a bloody newspaper." She realized that the piece would probably never see the printed page; it was just Bill covering himself for the slow days, but she had not been around long enough to turn down ideas.

She collected a package of clippings and took them back to her desk. It took her half an hour to find what she was looking for. Some of the clippings were so old that they crumbled in her hand.

Others, in the days before electronic typesetting, stained her fingers with ink. She grimaced. It seemed slightly bizarre for ancient ink telling of age-old murders to soil one's hands. Then she smiled. Someone, years ago, had done her work for her. A two-page spread was headed:

A Tragic Dynasty:
The Curse of the Thorn Family.

She stared at the photograph of a dagger with Christ on the hilt, grinned, and reached for her pen.

Much of the article was irrelevant for her purposes, the writer concentrating on the Thorn family, but she read it with increasing interest.

The untimely death yesterday of Damien Thorn, who, at thirty-two, was the youngest American ambassador to Britain, is the final chapter in a tragic story of the Thorn family, a dynasty which seemed to have everything, but whose members were fated to meet early and often bizarre ends.

Damien Thorn died in his bed of a heart attack. That, in itself, was unusual.

She glanced at the photograph of Thorn and at a succession of smaller photos, each with a caption: Robert Thorn, Damien's father, shot dead on the steps of a London church, the mystery killer never apprehended. Katherine, his mother had fallen to her death from a hospital window following an accident in the family home of Pereford which had caused her to miscarriage. Richard and Ann Thorn, Damien's uncle and aunt, disappeared without trace after the Thorn Museum was destroyed by fire; his half-brother Mark, dead at thirteen of a brain hemorrhage.

The article was split into sections. One was headed:

PEREFORD, STATELY HOME OF HORROR

Beneath a photograph of a country mansion was the story of Damien's young nanny, who had hanged herself from a window. Her successor was later found gruesomely murdered, on the night of Robert Thorn's death. And it was at Pereford, the writer reminded his readers, that Katherine Thorn had had the fall that eventually led to her death.

Arother section told of deaths outside the family. A man called Atherton, chief executive at Thorn Industries, had drowned during an ice-hockey match at the Thorn mansion in Chicago. He had fallen through the ice during a party to celebrate Damien's thirteenth birthday.

Another Thorn executive, named Pasarian, had

died in his laboratory while Damien and his school friends were on a guided tour of the plant. A woman reporter was killed under bizarre circumstances after interviewing Richard Thorn. Instinctively, as she read this, Carol Wyatt made the sign of the cross, provoking sniggers from a couple of messenger boys, but she paid them no attention.

The curator of the Thorn Museum had died after an accident at a railway yard. That same evening, the Thorn Museum in Chicago had burned to the ground. The list seemed endless. She rubbed her eyes, smudging her face with her ink-stained fingers and continued . . .

Ardrew Doyle, Damien's immediate predecessor at the U.S. embassy in London, had committed suicide in his office. No motive ever discovered. . . .

An unidentified man burned to death in a television studio while Damien was being interviewed. . . .

Two men, also unidentified, found dead in the area of a hunt in Cornwall which Damien had attended. A dagger was found in the hand of one man and near the body of the other. . . .

She made notes. These were the only deaths relevant to her story. The writer had drawn no conclusions about the accidents, merely pointing out that tragedy constantly surrounded the Thorns, moving with them and among them like a virus. She photocopied the clippings and then rang the press office at Scotland Yard. Within half an hour she was buying drinks in The Feathers.

The young press officer was glad to help. It was

not often that he had the chance of a beer with someone like Carol Wyatt. Normally his days were spent with cynical crime reporters who thought they were Philip Marlowe.

He glanced at the photograph and winced. "Offensive-looking weapon," he said.

"Do you have them in the museum?"

"Yep. Five of them. I checked the files."

She blinked. Maybe there was more to this than she had thought.

Minutes later they were standing by a glass case in the room in Scotland Yard known as the Black Museum. Each of the daggers was labeled, the five faces of Christ gazing up at them through the glass.

"The other three were found in another anonymous stiff in a chapel somewhere," the young man said, glancing at a file. "Cornwall again. Apparently we were brought in to investigate, which is why they are all here."

"Can I see the file?"

He handed it to her. "One dagger was found in his pocket, the other two were stuck in his back. . . . Now, then, what about a bite of lunch?"

"No, thanks," she said, smiling sweetly. "Got to get back."

Back at the office she pushed open James Richard's door.

"Is he in?"

Richard's secretary, a bossy woman who guarded Richard jealously, glared at her.

"Who are you?"

"A mere reporter. Where is he?"

"El Vino," she said, "but he's with—"

"Thanks," Carol said, and slammed the door.

She found him deep in conversation at the wine bar. It was a masculine establishment where women were permitted entry under strict rules of conduct. They were not allowed to stand at the bar or order drinks. She pushed her way through the crowd of lunchtime drinkers and smiled up at him, wished him good morning.

He blinked at her.

"Carol Wyatt," she prompted. "From the newsroom. We met once. May I have a quick word?"

He excused himself and moved toward the back with her.

"Sorry to butt in," she said, "but I'm doing a feature and I thought you might be able to point me in the right direction."

"If I can," he said.

"Bill told me that you had dinner with Philip Brennan in Rome—"

"That was a private matter," Richard said.

She handed him the copy of the article. "Would that be the dagger he was talking about?"

He peered at it. "I believe so. He mentioned something about the hilt being in that shape, but you're not to go bothering him, my dear. I don't want you to—"

But she had gone with a quick thanks thrown over her shoulder.

She wrote the feature on the five daggers quickly and impatiently, handed it in, and picked up the phone. The press attaché at the American embassy told her that if she wanted to see the ambassador, then she must go through normal channels, which meant a written request with a list of questions.

"Consider it done," she said cheerily, reaching for the company notepaper. Within half an hour, a dispatch rider was on his way to Grosvenor Square with her letter. She leaned back in her seat and smiled to herself; so, she was breaking protocol, so what? If her boss complained that she was doing something without consulting him, or if Richard got nasty, then she would smile and plead inexperience and youthful impetuosity. If she could establish some connection between the dagger in Rome and the unsolved deaths, then it was worth the risk; it would be a real story, not some rehashed old clippings job.

"Private dinner," she muttered. "Supercilious sod."

The next morning she was up early. It was her day off and she knew exactly what she was going to do with it. She had looked up Pereford in *English Stately Homes*; one of the grandest country homes in the land, the writer had claimed, a seventeenth-century residence set in four hundred acres of parkland with sixty-three rooms and two wings. An annex, built in the 1930s, had been tastefully designed and did not detract from the appearance of the estate; a trout stream, tennis courts, and vegetable garden . . .

It took her an hour to find the place. As she drew closer, she began to conjure up images in her mind of haunted castles, of Transylvanian mountaintops, trying to frighten herself, but she could not do it. The summer sun was shining, larks were singing; her imagination, she told herself, was not strong enough, and she was giggling as she drove past the big gates.

She braked and reversed, gazed at the gates, peered up the drive, then let out the clutch and eased the little car along the road. She drove for a mile one way, and a mile and a half the other, climbing all the time, then left the car on the shoulder and wandered across a field. There, below her, was the house. She gazed at it, wondering how many years of writing about daggers it would take just to pay one month's mortgage on a place like that.

The wall was ten feet high, but there were cracks in the brickwork. She gazed up at it. For a moment, she thought that maybe she should just turn around and go home, wait for the interview with the ambassador, and see what happened. But she itched with curiosity about the place. What harm would there be in having a look? If she was discovered, as she surely would be, she would claim that she thought it was just a park wall, plead ignorance again, and flash the disarming smile.

She wedged one foot in a crack, reached for a handhold, and hoisted herself up.

The buzzing of the alarm system startled the boy. He reached for the closed-circuit TV button, pressed it, and watched the young woman on the screen, sitting astride the wall. For a full minute she sat motionless, as if deciding something, then slithered down and dropped neatly onto the grass. He felt the hairs rise on the back of his neck and heard the dog move. It was staring through the window, the hackles raised, growling deep in its throat, its muzzle twitching, showing its teeth.

He touched its shoulder and it looked up at him, waiting for the order, but he pressed his fingers into the fur and held on to it. The dog's forehead creased as if in a frown, then it turned and looked up at the screen, panting, the saliva dripping onto the carpet.

The boy reached forward and adjusted the television to close-up, gazing intently as the woman began to move across the lawn, walking purposefully, as if she were on a country hike.

He stared at the big eyes and sniffed the air, his fingers and toes curling, his grip tightening on the dog until it yelped and still he held on to it, oblivious to everything except the image on the screen. She had crossed the outer limits of the estate now and her face was blurred as she pushed her way through the shrubbery. A branch, snapping back, stung her face, and she stopped. He could see the tears in her eyes and her chin tremble as she put her hand to her face and he felt a strange emotion. He felt that he wanted to brush the tears away and comfort her. The dog grunted at him and he sat back, watching fascinated as she moved forward again. He played with the focus and now she was moving slowly, picking her feet up through the shrubbery, stepping high like a dancer.

Soon she would be within a couple of hundred yards of the house. He jumped to his feet, ran out of the room, along the corridor, and down the stairs, the dog snuffling at his heels. Without stopping to think, he ran to the side door, pulled it open, and stumbled out onto the patio, moving toward the lawn, realizing as he ran that if he showed himself to her she could not be permitted to leave the estate.

She stepped out of the shrubbery onto manicured grass. The house was magnificent and there seemed to be no sign of movement. She could imagine moonlight parties, men in tailcoats and women in ball gowns. It looked like the sort of place where a young man could sip champagne from a young woman's slipper and neither would feel foolish. Again she giggled. Her imagination was getting the better of her. She touched her face where the branch had hit her, and rubbed her eyes. When she opened them, she saw a young man standing by the trees. She caught her breath, her hand fluttering to her mouth like a schoolgirl's.

He was quite the most beautiful creature she had ever seen.

"Hello," she offered, a broken squeak of a greeting.

He nodded; he was looking at her silently. She smiled and walked up to him, and he stepped out of the tree line into her path.

"Who are you?" he asked.

She could not place the accent, a deep voice, what they once called mid-Atlantic.

"My name's Carol. Who are you?"

"What are you doing here?"

"Just looking around the park." She smiled, but there was no reaction. Men normally responded to her in some way, either positively or gruffly, to cover up the sexual attraction, but he just stared unblinking.

"This isn't a park."

"Oh, I thought—"

"This is a private estate."

"Oh, really?"

She waited for the accusation of trespass and stood firm, feet planted square, ready for him. No boy, however handsome, however overpowering, would get the better of her.

"Would you like to see the house?"

"Thank you, yes . . ." The invitation was so unexpected that she stammered, then followed him as he crossed the lawn. As they reached the door, she stopped again, staring into the eyes of the dog, which had come around the side of the building. It growled, hackles raised. The boy looked at it and the growling stopped.

Carol shivered. "I've never seen such a—"

"It's a rottweiler," he said, interrupting her. "Once, they were used as drovers. And they hunt. They are fast over fifty yards, then they tire, but if they catch something in that time, a stag even . . ." He smiled and she turned away from him.

"I hate blood sports," she said.

"Yes," he said. "You would."

She followed him inside, the dog padding silently behind them, and she wrinkled her nose at the smell of it.

She stopped in the center of the hall and gazed around, her mouth open, looking up at the gallery, at plants hanging from baskets, thinking that it was from there that Katherine Thorn had fallen. It was a wonder she survived, she thought, glancing at the tiles.

Again she was conscious of the boy's penetrating gaze.

"Take a look around," he said, and ran up the stairs, leaving her with the dog.

"Thanks very much." She felt slightly bewildered, then turned and looked at the dog. It was gazing at her with the same dead stare.

So, she thought, this is where it all happened. It was hardly her idea of a haunted house. She crossed the hall toward the drawing room and looked inside, then turned and glanced again up the stairs, wondering where the boy had gone. She decided that she would charm him, ask him if he lived here and what he did for a living, find out what he knew about the house's history. She had got inside and now she was going to enjoy herself.

She spun on one heel. The dog had gone. She was on her own.

The boy stood motionless in the chapel staring into his father's eyes, his lips twitching in silent prayer. He reached for the hands and held them.

"Forgive me, Father, for my unworthiness," he said softly.

He stepped back, turned, and glared at the effigy of Christ.

"So," he sneered, "you continue with your squalid skulduggery. You send your soft-bellied seductress to flutter and preen before me, just as you sent my mother to my father. You tempt me as you tempted him into false emotions. You try to weaken my spirit with pious pity and counterfeit lust."

He moved around to the back of the cross and placed both hands on the hilt of the dagger, gripping it until the blade creaked in the wood.

"And this is the result," he snarled, drawing the dagger out. For a moment he stared at it, then moved back to the corpse, walked around it, and ran his fingers down the spine. Beneath the fifth vertebra was a deep wound. He touched it gently with fluttering fingers and looked again at the dagger.

"The seductress turned murderer," he whispered. "This is what happened when my father turned his back." For a moment he stood in silence, then leaped at the effigy, struck the face with his fist, then drove the dagger once more into the spine, grunting with the effort.

"You think you learned about temptation," he said, moving around to stare into the face. "You think you conquered temptation, but your forty days and forty nights taught you nothing. You send me this creature to turn me away from my destiny, to guide me toward your straight and narrow path, that cul-de-sac of endeavor and ambition."

He shook his head. "But you have failed, as you will always fail."

He spread one hand over the face.

"You, who were born of a virgin, while I . . ." He left the sentence unfinished and turned away.

"Get thee behind me, Nazarene," he whispered.

She had seen enough. The sun had gone down and she could detect the first chill of evening. Her nostrils twitched and she grimaced at the smell of decay. The scent of the dog was everywhere, but there was no sign of the boy. She felt shivery, the thin blouse and summer skirt no longer sufficient. Suddenly she wanted to be out of the house, back to her car and away from here.

She opened the door and stepped out into the drive, stumbling as one of the heels of her shoes snapped. She took them off and walked slowly across the drive, the sharp gravel causing her to wince. A wind had risen, and when she reached the lawn, she had the feeling that she was being watched. She looked back, expecting to see the dog, but there was nothing. She padded across the lawn to the shrubbery and began to run, and still the stench of the dog seemed to be clinging to her, bringing to mind a flash of memory, of her eighteenth birthday when she had drunk too much champagne and was sick and had to walk home in the rain, the stench of vomit making her retch. And now it was the same. The farther she ran from the house, the stronger the stench became.

She pushed her way through the shrubbery, stumbling between bushes. Twice she tripped on roots and almost fell. It had grown dark with the suddenness of a tropical nightfall. She was no longer sure of her bearings. As she ran, the branches lashed against her face and stung her eyes. In her nightmares she was always being chased and she would wake up trembling. She hated it, the very idea of being hunted, so much so that she could not watch a movie that contained a chase sequence.

She stopped. Ahead, the shrubbery was thinning out. Beyond would be the rough grass and then the wall and her little car. She ran toward the tree line, pushed past more branches, and stopped again. There was another shrubbery. She frowned, puzzled, thinking that she must have run in a circle. She cursed. She never did have any sense of direction.

Again she shivered and clutched herself, arms around her chest, running blind through the shrubs toward the open space. If she kept going, she must come to the wall. It stood to reason. What was the size of the estate? Four hundred acres? Sooner or later she would find the wall and leave Pereford behind.

The dog had stalked her silently, keeping fifty ⸱⸱⸱ behind, stopping when she stopped, then padding after her, moving slowly, conserving its energy. Through the shrubbery it gained on her until by the time she had reached open ground, it was thirty yards behind her. Again it stopped, sniffing the air, watching the woman run across the rough grass, then it leaped forward, the great chest heaving, running at a gallop, gaining on her with every yard . . .

There was no sound, only the increasing stench. She did not hear it until it was almost upon her. She turned as it leaped at her, hitting her with its massive head, butting her at waist level and knocking her to the ground. She had no time to scream. As she tried to get to her feet, the dog was upon her, the jaws snapping shut on her ankle. It shook its head violently, the jaws clamped shut, the teeth tearing at bone and gristle; only then did she scream. Briefly the dog gazed at her, then lumbered off into the night, lay in the grass a few yards from her, and watched. . . .

The scream died in her throat as she pressed her face into the grass, her fingers scratching at the earth, gripping at something as she fought the agony. She knew that the tendon had snapped, the tension sending it zipping up her calf into the back of her knee. The pain made her retch and the retching, in turn, increased her agony. She tried to struggle onto her good leg, but she could not move.

Slowly she scrawled forward, biting her bottom lip so that it bled, trying to fight pain with pain.

If she could reach the wall, then she could shout for help. Someone, surely, would find her.

It took her an hour to move ten yards, and together from downwind, the boy and the dog watched her. For another hour she called for help, then she lay still and sobbed into the grass.

Soon the sobbing stopped and the boy moved on all fours toward her. As he approached, she moved again, raising her head a couple of inches and trying to look behind her. The boy stopped. It was almost dawn before she was completely still and only then did he move closer.

Her dreams had been of scavengers, of jackals and hyenas and vultures, and of men from a movie she had once seen, slitting the hamstrings of their prisoners so that they could not escape. She opened her eyes and stared at the ground, at the patch of dried saliva where she had dribbled. Her fingers were raw from scratching at the earth, but at least her leg was numb now, and that was something. She raised her head and again the pain zipped through her, then she turned and looked over her shoulder into the eyes of the boy. He was naked, crawling toward her. She tried to smile, tried to speak, but she could not make a sound and she thought that maybe all this was part of the nightmare. His eyes seemed narrow with a yellow tint and his breath was foul, like that of the dog. He was leaning over her body now and she whimpered, trying to understand what he was doing to her. She could feel his teeth sharp on the ᵇ ᵗ ᶜ her neck, nibbling, as if he were searching for something. She opened her mouth to scream and the last thing she heard was his grunt of satisfaction as his jaw snapped on the cervical nerve; then there was nothing.

Chapter 6

Carol Wyatt's instincts had proved to be correct. Her piece on the daggers did not appear in the paper, being held as stock for a quiet day, but through the syndication department it turned up in a number of magazines throughout the world, and within a week of her death, an old man in Chicago saw it and dropped his coffeecup from trembling fingers.

He read the article quickly, then made a call to his priest. That done, he went to his study and pored over his books, refreshing his memory and feeding his curiosity. Shaking with excitement, he telephoned the magazine and was given a London number. As he placed the call, he began to feel bold and impetuous, like a private detective.

He checked the by-line on the magazine again and was put through to the news desk.

"My name is Michael Finn," he said. "From Chicago. May I speak to one of your reporters, please? Carol Wyatt."

"I wish you could," said a male voice. "She's bee· missing for a week. Could you tell me what · ·nnection with?"

As he spoke, there was a tap on the door and a small, thin man looked in. He was wearing a gray suit and a clerical collar. Finn beckoned to him to come in, pointed to a seat. When he had finished his call, he turned and shook the priest's hand, then with a dramatic flourish, he handed over the magazine.

The priest read it slowly. "Well, now," he said eventually. "Isn't that a strange thing?"

"Very," said Finn.

For a while they reminisced about the day when Finn had stumbled upon the daggers at an uptown auction and how the priest had taken them to Italy, to a monastery at Subiaco.

"If we had known," said the priest. "We should have left them where they were."

"Think back," said Finn. "The Italian gave no clue as to what he was going to do with them?"

"None."

Finn shook his head in astonishment, unable to rid himself of the feeling that he had been responsible for the deaths of the men mentioned in the magazine.

"Do you know if this De Carlo is still alive?"

The priest shrugged. "I've no idea, but you could call the monastery."

Finn nodded, again feeling impetuous. "If he is alive, will you come with me to see him?"

"Why? What would it achieve?"

"It would satisfy curiosity."

The priest shook his head. "My curiosity is not so great. Besides, I have a flock to attend."

"Of course," said Finn. "But I'm due a vacation,

and what could be nicer than Rome at this time of year?"

"Quite," said the priest.

In all his sixty years Finn had rarely left the boundaries of his native city. His life had been books and the study of ancient history. He was acknowledged as an expert, with one of the most comprehensive collections of biblical texts in the country, the prize exhibit being one of the Dead Sea Scrolls, the cracked papyrus safe from further damage in a glass case in his study. He was a respected scholar, but he knew little of the modern world, and as he strapped himself into his seat on the aircraft, he felt exhilarated.

He had enjoyed packing, he had enjoyed the sweet pang of farewell from his wife, and he was looking forward to a scent of mystery and perhaps of danger. As the aircraft built up speed for take-off, he felt young again, as if the cobwebs had been blown from his brain and the dust swept from his soul. He even broke a longtime habit by taking a cocktail from the stewardess before it was even dark.

He wasted no time at Rome, hiring a car from the airport desk and setting off immediately east toward Subiaco. There would be time enough to see the sights after he had met De Carlo. He drove for an hour into the twilight, checking his map, and he saw the monastery before he realized he was upon it, a ruin of a building on a hilltop, built f black stone.

seemed to be no light, no windows. Finn

shivered, feeling, as Father Doolan had before him, a sense of history and continuity, something that could only be imagined in Chicago.

He stopped the car and shut off the engine, conscious of total silence. As he padded up the worn path toward the heavy oak door, his lips moved in silent prayer. He who had spent his life in libraries had come upon the real thing, a place where such knowledge had been distilled over the centuries. He felt small and suddenly insignificant.

He climbed worn flagstones and began to pick up the low monotone of men at prayer. He rapped a heavy iron knocker and the sound echoed through the building but did not disturb the chanted prayers. He waited a full minute before the door was opened. A monk, his face almost hidden by a cowl, looked at him in silence. Finn introduced himself and the monk stood back to let him enter.

"We are pleased you have come." The monk's English was clear.

"I hope I'm not intruding."

"Father De Carlo will be happy to see you. No one visits him now."

"How is he?"

"His soul is in torment."

Finn followed the monk down a passage and along a narrow corridor. The place smelled and tasted of damp, and he shivered.

The monk stopped at a door, knocked, and pushed it open. Finn entered the tiny room and saw an old man on a narrow bed. Doolan had

71

described the priest as a heavily built man with a strong face, high cheekbones, an aquiline nose, and although Finn had been prepared for a change, he had not expected to see such deterioration. The skin had shrunk around the skull and his movements were slow and obviously painful as he pushed himself into a sitting position.

Finn searched for an introduction.

"I'm sorry to find you unwell—"

"I am well," said De Carlo. "It is the world that is sick."

"Ah. Yes." Finn, slightly nonplussed, turned and smiled as the young monk brought him a chair. He perched on the edge of it and reached into his pocket for Carol Wyatt's article.

"You received my letter?"

The priest nodded. "When you found the daggers, did you know their significance?"

"Only that they were similar to drawings of some I had seen and that they may have come from the ancient city of Megiddo."

"That is correct. From the underground city near Jerusalem, the place once known as Armageddon."

"And that they might have had some sort of historical significance," Finn continued. "I believe that they may once have been used in a form of exorcism."

De Carlo smiled. "A poor word, meaning the casting out of devils. No. They are far more important."

Finn held out the article. "I had almost forgotten about them, until I came across this."

De Carlo squinted and looked at it, then as he read the article, tears came to his eyes. He brushed them aside with his sleeve and looked up again at Finn.

"I want you to listen to what I am going to tell you and I do not want you to interrupt me."

Finn nodded and sat back as the priest slowly began his narrative.

He told how in that very room, as a novice, he had been present at the dying confession of a priest called Spiletto, a priest who had become a disciple of the devil and who had officiated at a diabolical birth, a creature born of an abominable union of the devil with a jackal.

Finn blinked but said nothing.

After the creature had been made presentable, it was substituted for a newly born human child, the son of Robert and Katherine Thorn. The father was told only that his child had died and that God wished him to bring up a foundling as his own. Katherine Thorn had had a history of miscarriages and this was the last chance for her to have a child. Robert Thorn agreed. He told his wife that the substitute was their son. They called him Damien.

"The child was a force of destruction," said De Carlo. "Eventually Robert Thorn realized the truth. He went to Megiddo and was given the seven daggers, but before he could destroy the child, he was himself killed."

Finn rubbed his eyes and De Carlo gestured to the monk to bring him a glass of water, then went on to tell him how Damien Thorn had grown to become head of the Thorn Corporation, a company that controlled the feeding of much of the world's population, how he surrounded himself with disciples, how his power and influence grew. . . .

"Then my prayers were answered," De Carlo continued. "You found the daggers. Your priest brought them to me. It was the will of God. You acted as God's instrument."

Finn gulped the water but said nothing.

"With six of my brothers I traveled to England to destroy Damien Thorn." He reached beneath his cot and held up a dagger. Instinctively Finn drew back, away from the glint of the steel and the unique carving on the hilt. It was the same dagger and quite suddenly it occurred to him that if this crazy priest were telling the truth, then he, Michael Finn, might be accused of being an accessory to murder.

"You, a priest, were going to kill a man?" he said incredulously.

"He was not a man," said De Carlo in a flat monotone. "He was the Antichrist."

Finn grunted, a choking chuckle, as De Carlo held the dagger in front of his face.

"I know it is hard for you to accept," he said. "Even you, a man of faith. It was harder for Robert Thorn to accept, but eventually he did. So too did a woman called Kate Reynolds. It was she who drove this dagger into Damien Thorn's back." He laid it on Finn's lap and the old man gazed down at the face of Christ.

"I thought we had succeeded, that we had

destroyed him. But it was a false dawn." De Carlo sighed and lay back on the cot.

Finn touched the blade and tried to stand up. He wanted to be out of this place, but there was no strength in his legs.

"You know the Book of Revelation?" asked the priest.

Finn nodded.

" 'And it was given unto him to make war with the saints, and to overcome them,' " said De Carlo. " 'And power was given him over all kindreds, and tongues, and nations.' " He paused. " 'Power was given unto him,' " he repeated. "There is nothing more powerful on earth than the Thorn Corporation."

Finn shook his head. "You can interpret the Bible any way you wish."

"Indeed," said De Carlo. "And the disciples of the Antichrist have made their interpretation. There was a man called Tassone who helped at the diabolical birth. Later he repented and pointed out to Robert Thorn that the time was at hand. The Jews had returned to the promised land. Throughout the world there was famine. Politics was in disarray. 'And he shall set up an ensign for the nations and gather together the dispersed of Judah from the four corners of the earth.' "

He looked at Finn. "You know the Bible and the interpretations. That in the final days Christ will be reborn and will have to face the Antichrist, that Armageddon will be fought over Israel."

Finn nodded.

"He is risen. I have seen Him."

Finn passed a hand over his brow. He wanted to be gone, but still he stayed, reluctantly fascinated.

"Thorn instructed his disciples to kill all the male babies born on the day Christ was reborn. A hundred were murdered but the Christ Child was unharmed."

Finn rubbed his eyes and the priest reached out to him, gently touched his arm.

"I know," he said. "It is too much for a man to take, especially one like you, to whom all this has been the stuff of libraries. But please bear with me."

He reached for a shelf above his bed, took down two envelopes, and handed one to Finn.

"Read this letter first. It was written by a brave woman from her sickbed. Read it and believe."

The address of the sender was northwest London. Finn turned to the last page and glanced at the signature. The name meant nothing to him.

"Read it," said De Carlo, and the words were a command.

Finn turned back to the beginning and read in silence:

Next week, Father, I am due to enter a clinic for an abdominal operation. I have been told that the convalescence will be long and painful. I do not believe this. I do not think that I will survive. As you know better than most, I am hardly a dramatic individual, still less am I melodramatic, so you can accept that this is not the neurotic ravings of a demented woman. I have simply looked at the evidence—my body—and felt the pain and come to the obvious conclusion.

You are the one person I can write to, the only one who knows the horror. The pains began a few weeks after you left England. At first I ignored them until I noticed a swelling. My doctor sent me to a specialist who has been taking regular tests as the swelling increases. He does not say the word "cancer," of course. Even these days, it is a taboo word. He talks vaguely of "growths" and shows me X rays.

However, I do not believe the "growth" to be a tumour and I am convinced that the X rays are not mine. Father, the damned growth *kicks*. If this is a nightmare, then it is a waking nightmare.

I never told you that, in your phraseology, Damien and I were "one flesh." There was nothing to be gained by telling you, but if I do not come out of this clinic, then this letter is, I suppose, a substitute for confession. You would not be reading it unless I were already dead.

I am not a believer, in spite of your so-called evidence about Damien. I still cannot accept it. All I know is that a man named Damien Thorn tried to take my son from me, that he stabbed him, and that I, in turn, killed him. I can still hear the obscene suction as I pulled the dagger from Peter's back and the grating sound as I drove it into Damien's spine. That is all I know. To you, he is the Antichrist. To me he was an attractive man with a strange birthmark—no more than that.

However there are moments in the night when I get visions that this thing inside me is evil, that it is . . . But I won't continue. You are the one with faith, the belief in devils and goblins and God knows what. I am also aware of soothing dreams and you will say it is the Son of God comforting me. I don't know. All I know is that I am due to go the clinic. Pray for me, Father De Carlo. At the very least, your prayers can do me no harm. If I am wrong, if my scepticism turns out to be cynicism, then your prayers may do me some good.

Finn looked at the priest.

"Turn the page," said De Carlo.

Finn did as he was asked. Scrawled on the back was a postscript.

I have lain with the devil, Father. I have bruised my breasts and committed the most original sin imaginable. Pray for my soul. Please.

"The postscript is dated on the morning she went into the clinic," said De Carlo. "She died the next day. The letter was sent to me from her solicitor's office."

Finn shook his head. "Poor woman. Will they never find a cure for cancer?"

"It was not cancer."

Finn looked at him and blinked.

"She was Damien Thorn's final victim. I believe that she gave birth to his child." He handed over the second letter.

Finn took it without speaking. Again he began to read, his lips forming the words:

"Forgive me, Father, for I have sinned . . ."

When he had finished, he looked again at De Carlo. There was no color in his face.

"This is nonsense," he said.

De Carlo shook his head. "Why would she lie?"

"She is not lying. She is mad."

"No. That conclusion is the easy way out. She was not lying. She was sane, for the first time since the devil reached out for her."

Finn leaned forward to speak, but De Carlo raised a hand for silence. "On that terrible night, Kate Reynolds and I buried the body of her son and left the body of Damien Thorn to molder on the altar. I brought the dagger with me, and a belief in a new dawn. But it was a false dawn. The apostates of the devil found the body. They said it was a heart attack. Their own doctor confirmed it. He was supposedly buried in the family plot in Chicago."

"I know," said Finn eagerly. "I saw it on television."

De Carlo took the letter from him, his finger moving along an underlined paragraph. " 'Each knife must be buried to the hilt,' " he read slowly.

" 'Planted to form the sign of the cross. The first dagger is the most important. It extinguishes physical life and forms the center of the cross. The subsequent placements extinguish spiritual life. It must be done on hallowed ground. We, the disciples, were taught this so that we might be the more vigilant in preventing it.' "

De Carlo sighed and lay back. "All we did was destroy the body of the Antichrist. His spirit is unharmed, working through the abomination that is his son." He closed his eyes and spoke almost in a whisper. "I awoke on the day it was excreted into the world and I knew then that I had failed and that all my brothers had died in vain, but only in the last month, when this letter arrived, did I realize our mistake. It was ignorance. We simply did not know."

Finn slowly got to his feet, his knees trembling. He felt dizzy and suddenly very old.

De Carlo opened his eyes. "I have written all this down, all that I have told you. Take my notes and the letters. Go to London and see the American ambassador. He will help."

"Why?" Finn said. "Why should he?"

"He is a man of integrity. He also has power and influence. He can get hold of the daggers. He can do what you cannot. He is also young. You, like me, are old and feeble. Though your spirit may be willing, your flesh . . ." He smiled and left the sentence unfinished as he painfully pushed himself off the bed and reached for his Bible.

"Promise me," he said.

Finn opened his mouth to speak but no words came. De Carlo reached for his hand and placed it on the Bible.

"Promise me, for the love of God."

Finn nodded. "I promise."

"Then kneel with me."

Together, in the cramped cell they knelt, De Carlo praying in Latin, Finn wondering what he had done. As they got to their feet, the priest placed his hands on Finn's shoulders.

"Persuade the ambassador. When he is ready, I will send the dagger to him." He smiled. "The risen Christ will guide you. Trust in Him, and pray to Him. He walks the earth once more. I know. I have seen Him."

Finn collected the notes and the letters and made for the door. As he reached it, he realized that one question remained. "What happened to the first child?" he asked. "The real Thorn child?"

"Murdered," said De Carlo flatly. "The first of many."

Finn shivered, and it was not until he had driven away and the monastery was out of sight that the shivering stopped and the doubts began.

Chapter 7

The call was person-to-person from Rome. Father Thomas Doolan waited expectantly, an absurd thought going through his mind that he was being rung up by the Vatican, and he was mildly disappointed to hear the voice of Michael Finn. By the time he had replaced the receiver he was cursing himself for his weakness. He gazed at the crucifix on the wall and wondered what made him agree to do such a thing. It was a kind of sacrilege. Maybe it was even against the law.

But, he argued, Finn had always been a good friend to the Church. It was due almost entirely to the influence of Michael Finn that the roof was still in good repair.

But there was still the organ. There was always something breaking down or falling to pieces. Thomas Doolan was a practical man who knew where God's bread was buttered. Saving souls needed financial backing, so he would do what the man in Rome asked of him.

He called the number Finn had given him and the voice at the other end was only too pleased to help. It took him an hour in a cab to find the address, pick up the machine, and drive back to the cemetery on the North Side. He paid off the cab and stood by the gate, studying the machine that Finn's friend had lent him. It had a broad spoon-shaped base, a three-feet shaft, and a handle in which was set a dial and a color TV screen. The man had said proudly that it was the very latest of its kind and highly sensitive, an essential tool for geologists and amateur prospectors.

He adjusted the dial to six feet and switched it on. The machine hummed, and quite clearly on the screen he could make out the substrata of Chicago. He shook his head in wonder and glanced at the sky. It was a cloudless night. Mischievously he aimed the detector at the stars and squinted at the screen: nothing. The dial had a range of fifty feet. A pity, thought Doolan. If it could reach infinity, then maybe he could have spotted his Maker.

He switched it off, pushed open the cemetery gate, and walked in, shoving the detector in front of him like a lawn mower. The place was well-maintained, the last resting place of the Chicago rich. There was a waiting list for interment, something that did not appeal to Doolan's Irish soul and that knowledge made it easier for him to perform this minor act of sacrilege, if sacrilege it was.

The Thorn mausoleum stood by the lake, a circular building of imported granite, sparkling in the moonlight. The double oak doors were closed, but they opened to Doolan's touch, swinging back on oiled hinges to reveal the vault.

There was nothing elaborate about the place. The room was circular, studded with plaques and lit by a single flame flickering in an alcove. There was no graffiti, he noticed. It was one of the few buildings in the city free of the usual scrawling.

He walked around the room, reading the plaques that marked the coffins of the Thorn family, going back four generations. The largest was commemorative.

"To the memory of Robert and Katherine Thorn," he read. "Buried together in New York City. And to Richard and Ann Thorn. May their souls rest in peace."

He stepped back, turned and gazed at a large marble slab set in the center of the floor. It was engraved:

DAMIEN THORN
1950–1982

There was no epitaph, just the name. Even in death Damien dominated the place. Doolan remembered the ceremony well. He had seen it on the news, the pallbearers carrying the coffin onto the mausoleum, then the doors closing on the cameras while the newscaster talked about the tragedy of his death.

He switched on the machine and felt a shiver chase itself up his spine. He had attended and officiated at countless interments, and he wanted to walk away, to let the body rest at peace, but he gripped the handle and told himself to get on with it. The job would not take long and then he would be away.

He glanced at the screen, at a mass of brown earth. He adjusted the dial to five feet and it came into sharp focus, an X-ray picture of clay, reminding Doolan of a chocolate bar, undisturbed and smooth, exactly as it had been laid down millions of years ago.

He moved toward the slab and stood over the grave, his feet planted on the name of the deceased. Again he looked at the screen. The texture of the clay had changed. It was disturbed and pitted with pebbles. He placed it directly between his feet and turned the dial, selecting short-range focus. He moved it to five feet one inch, then five feet two, sucking in breath as the mahogany lid of the coffin appeared on the screen. Instinctively, with his free hand he made the sign of the cross as a crazy thought zipped through his brain, a story he had heard that the hair and the nails continued to grow after death, and he wondered if he was going to gaze down at a mass of beard and talons.

He closed his eyes and touched the dial, then forced himself to look again. The screen showed rocks, a neat layer, a flat rockery. He frowned and moved the dial; two inches up, more rocks; down four inches, the floor of the coffin; up eight inches, and the screen went blank, then flashed two words at him: AIR VENT.

He moved quickly, passing the scanner across the slab and a couple of feet on either side until he was satisfied. But for a pile of rocks, the coffin of Damien Thorn was empty. He snapped the machine off and stared stupidly at the inscription, shook his head, and stepped off the slab.

"What I need," he said aloud, "is a large drink."

Far to the east, the boy stood in his chapel, gripping the hands of his father, his lips moving soundlessly; the perspiration ran into his eyes and down his arms into his palms, until the hands of Damien Thorn were moist. The boy's face was set in a frown of concentration, the veins on his temples standing out like wire, while below in the Pereford woods, the massive dog raised its head to the western sky and howled into the night. . . .

The bartender at O'Lunney's, a place near the North Chicago cemetery, was not given to wondering about the oddities of human behavior and paid little attention to the thin man with the metal detector under his arm who was downing shots of rye like Prohibition was coming back. Twice he saw him go to the phone and return, shaking his head, to the counter.

Another belt of booze and he was off again; phoning the wife, the bartender speculated, making excuses.

Doolan hit the Operator buttor.

"Person-to-person collect call to Rome, Italy," he said.

"Just one moment."

"Please, this time," he whispered, "don't let the

lines be busy." He needed to pass on the information quickly, to share the responsibility of his discovery. He read out the number and waited.

"Your number's ringing."

"Thank God."

He muttered to himself, drumming his fingers on the wall.

"Your party's room doesn't answer."

"Well, would you have him paged, please?"

"Just one moment."

It seemed an eternity until Finn came to the phone. Behind him someone burst into song and Doolan had to press his fingers over his ears as he told his story. Finn thanked him and Doolan could hear the excitement in the man's voice. He hung up and sagged against the wall; a last drink, he thought, then he would go home.

"So you're a priest?" said the bartender an hour later. "I hear a lot of confessions myself."

"Oh, yeah?" Doolan gazed at his glass and decided that one more would be too many. The booze had worked, he told himself. He had got over the shock. He would be able to sleep and not be bothered by nightmares.

He lurched out into the night and shivered. The weather had changed, a wind whipping across the lake, clouds scudding across the moon, building up from the east. He pushed open the cemetery gates—a shortcut, the bartender had said—to the nearest cabstand. He stumbled along a path, holding the detector across his chest like an Indian carrying a rifle. He belched, tasted bile, and spat, thinking that he should not have had so much rye and beer. He wasn't accustomed to it.

Briefly he glanced at the Thorn mausoleum and imagined he saw movement, pinpricks of yellow; then he turned toward the far gate, shivering, a vague nightmare of being chased flitting through his mind. He began to walk faster, head down against the wind, moving at a trot, but somehow he was not coordinated. He feet scuffed against the hedge and he stumbled against a gravestone; then he twitched, startled as the detector began to whirr. He fumbled for the switch to shut it off, but he could not find it and gazed at the screen. It had focused on the contents of the grave and a skull grinned up at him. Doolan blinked and swallowed, then turned and ran, dragging the machine behind him.

He wanted to keep running and not stop until he reached the gate, but there was no strength in him. He coughed and stumbled against a statue of an angel, shivered, and spat bile into the earth. He retched into the base of the statue and he could taste the rye and the beer. Groaning, he wiped his mouth with his sleeve, conscious again of the steady hum of the detector and the colors on the screen.

Reluctantly he stared at the screen and this time the skeleton was that of an animal. It looked, he thought, like a dog, or a hyena, or a jackal. As he got to his feet, he thought the bones moved, the back legs kicking out. He wanted to look away, but despite himself he was fascinated. The air was foul and he reached into his pocket for a handkerchief to cover his nose.

He pushed himself away from the statue and moved toward the gate. Peering forward, he could see nothing except a succession of gravestones. Murmuring a prayer, he stumbled between them, the detector in front of him, leading the way. It stopped by a double headstone and he leaned against it, panting; the inscription said:

JOHN AND MARTHA CARTWRIGHT;
AT PEACE TOGETHER FOR ETERNITY.

Their bones filled the screen. Martha and John, their bones intertwined. Maggots crawled between their ribs and flies buzzed around their faces. They were lying side by side in the coitus position, the man half on top of the woman. As Doolan stared at the screen, the skull of Martha Cartwright leered at him over her husband's shoulder, her tongue licked lasciviously around the gaping hole of her mouth, and he heard himself scream in a voice that was not his as he ran, blindly, still clutching the machine, running without thought. He crashed against gravestones and bruised his hip but felt nothing.

He was running and stumbling, screaming the same word over and over: "Sacrilege!" the sound echoing among the trees. As he ran, he shook his head violently, trying to rid his mind of the sight of the skull, but it was branded on his brain and in his panic he did not see the open grave.

He was conscious of a crack like a gunshot and the pain zipped up his arm. He tried to turn his head but he could not move. He spat clay and squinted up at the sheer wall of earth. Only his eyes moved. He could feel nothing in his legs. A spasm of panic shot through him, but he fought it, the pain in his wrist seeming to concentrate his mind. The paralysis would be temporary, he told himself, just a concussion. In a moment he would get the feeling back in his legs. He could just glimpse his arm, the hand at a grotesque angle. He had never broken a bone before. Briefly the panic gripped him again and he closed his eyes, murmuring a prayer. When he opened them, he could see a shape at the graveside. He squinted and focused. It was the head of a dog, a massive head, the yellow eyes glinting down at him. And now he realized why there was no graffiti around the mausoleum; the place was guarded at night by such dogs.

He stared into the dog's eyes and cackled hysterically. Maybe it would fetch help. He felt like a mountaineer caught in an avalanche. Maybe it was a Saint Bernard, he thought. Maybe it had a cask of brandy. Again the rye bubbled in his throat. He tried to belch but he could not. The sour liquid dribbled from the corner of his mouth; he tried to move his head away from the stench, but his muscles would no longer obey the messages from his brain.

He watched as the dog bent its snout into the mound of earth by the lip of the grave and he blinked as a shower of clay spattered onto his face and a pebble stung his eyebrow.

"Hey," he squealed.

The dog snuffled and scrabbled at the earth.

"Don't . . ." he shouted, but a lump of clay hit him on the throat and silenced him. He heard a grunt and saw a second dog at the graveside, then a third. Beyond them he could make out a rectangle of sky. The clouds had passed and he gazed at the stars, the cluster they called the Seven Sisters; then they vanished as the earth rained down on him again and he could hear the scraping of the dogs' paws as they scratched at the earth, pushing it back between their legs into the grave.

A piece of flint smashed into his nose and he felt the blood spurt. His mouth opened in an involuntary scream and filled with clay, and he closed his eyes tightly, feeling the earth spatter on his eyelids. All he could hope now was the dogs would take their time so that he could confess. He could not meet his Maker without giving himself the last rites. Silently he muttered to himself words of Latin he had been taught as a boy, while the earth built up around his lips and clogged his nostrils.

At first, in the early-morning light, the gravedigger thought that a small shrub had grown out of the new grave, a tiny five-stemmed pink shrub. He reached down to touch it, then backed away, moaning deep in his throat, almost tripping

over a machine like a lawn mower that lay at an
angle by the graveside, its motor whirring, the
face of Thomas Doolan, eyes and mouth tightly
shut, filling the screen.

Chapter 8

Seated by a window on the Rome-to-London shuttle flight, Michael Finn went over the conversation with the priest and tried to assemble his thoughts. He reached for his briefcase and looked again at the notes De Carlo had given him. Part of his brain rejected it and he was tempted to take the package to the back of the aircraft and flush it down the john, see it vanish in a blue whirlpool, forget all about it, and fly on home from London.

But he had made a promise, his hand on a Bible. He sighed and stared vacantly at the two letters nestling in his briefcase. Certainly the woman called Lamont was mad and the other terminally ill. De Carlo was probably senile. Yet Damien Thorn's body was not in its grave and that, at least, was worth investigating.

He reached for his Bible and a notebook. A lifetime of research had given him an intimate knowledge of the Scriptures and he had no difficulty finding the relevant references. He skimmed through the pages like a driver studying a road map, muttering to himself so that the woman next to him shifted in her seat and looked anxiously at him.

"A jubilee shall that fiftieth year be unto you," he murmured. He flipped on to the New Testament, scribbling in his notebook.

"For nation shall rise against nation and kingdom against kingdom . . . The last days," he said to himself. Again he thumbed the pages. "This generation will by no means pass away until all those things occur."

He put down his pencil and closed his eyes, thinking back to his youth, which had been a time of regular religious instruction. His adult life had been almost totally devoted to historical research. He was, by consequence, a man of deep faith with a scientist's curiosity, two elements he had never found to be contradictory, but as he dropped off to sleep, the fear that occasionally nagged him began to haunt him: the fear that the doomwatchers and the Cassandras were right and that the biblical predictions were about to be realized.

The Antichrist lived. The old priest had seen the reborn Christ. If De Carlo was not insane, then Armageddon was at hand.

Going through Customs and Immigration, he kept his mind fixed on minor details so that he would not have to think of what he had to do: Should he take a cab or the Underground? Which hotel should he use? Which one of his colleagues would he ring first? He picked up his baggage and moved through the concourse, stopped at a news-

paper stand, and searched in his pockets for
English coins.

The *International Herald-Tribune* was promi-
nently displayed. He bent to pick it up and
stopped, bent over, as if turned to stone, then
slowly took the paper off the shelf and
straightened, murmuring to himself, oblivious to
the swell of travelers around him, ignoring their
complaints that he was blocking the aisle.

A police lieutenant was quoted as saying that
the murder was one of the sickest he had come
across and wondered what kind of person would
bury a man alive, a man who, the pathologist said,
had broken his neck in the fall and would have
been totally paralyzed.

"Oh, my God," Finn whispered, and felt his
knees buckle. And then there were people around
him helping him up, asking him if he was okay, or
if he needed a doctor.

He checked into a small hotel near Piccadilly
and phoned home. He was affectionate toward his
wife, more affectionate than he could remember,
and when he hung up, he thought that she was
probably suspicious, thinking that he was acting
with a guilty conscience. When he got back, he
planned to take her in his arms and tell her how
much she meant to him. He could not wait to be
home, but first there was a promise to keep.

He decided to walk around London. Normally
a new city fascinated him, but he could not
concentrate. The face of Thomas Doolan kept in-

truding into his mind and he kept hearing his voice reluctantly agreeing to do him a favor; then, last night, that strange phone call, the slurred speech, nervous and excited, as if he had drunk too much.

Finn felt tears on his cheek and he wiped them away. He felt guilty, responsible for the man's death. He wiped his eyes and looked up, trying to discover where he was. He had stopped by a church and the door was open. Without thinking, he wandered inside.

As he knelt at the pew, he wondered how he was going to keep his promise to De Carlo. He could not get the daggers. If they had been in a museum or a private collection, then he might have stood a chance. He still had the original bill of sale. But Scotland Yard . . . They might as well be at the bottom of the ocean.

He tried to think what he might do. He was not the type of man for the job. He knew it. De Carlo had realized it. Maybe he could hire someone, a private investigator perhaps.

He shook his head and closed his eyes, feeling a chill of foreboding, an intimation of mortality. Then he remembered De Carlo's words: "The risen Christ will help you."

He prayed for the girl who had vanished, he prayed for the soul of Thomas Doolan, and lastly he prayed for himself.

Later he could not recall having entered the church. It was almost as if he had been led there, but when he left and found himself back in the street, he knew exactly what he had to do.

"Mr. Ambassador."

Brennan awoke suddenly and guiltily, the remnants of a dream fading from his mind. He had a crick in his neck. His hand was numb where his forehead had rested.

He pushed himself upright and snapped on the intercom button and grunted an acknowledgment.

"The briefing papers, sir."

"Thanks." His voice was still thick with sleep. "Send them in, will you?"

He yawned and made his way to the bathroom, splashed water on his face, and rubbed his eyes. Three times that week he had fallen asleep at his desk. It wasn't good enough. Somehow he was going to have to do something about Margaret's rediscovered sexual appetites.

"Bromide in her vodka," he said to his reflection, and grinned. Still, he thought, it was a nice problem to have.

The briefing papers from the State Department made, as usual, depressing reading. He went through them carefully, then picked up a note confirming his invitation to talks at the Foreign Office. Idly he wondered if, when they were over, he might manage a few days' vacation. He felt that he needed a break. But where?

Given you are a man of conscience, he told himself, where can you go? Half the world seemed to treat human rights as a joke, dissident behavior resulting in either jail sentences or a firing squad. This ruled out most of the Latin-American countries, Greece, and Turkey.

The Arab countries had either gone fundamentalist and reverted to the Middle Ages, or they had accepted the worst of Western ways with secret police forces and draconian powers of arrest. Spain again was flirting with fascism, as was Italy. The African continent was a mess of warring factions. The islands of the Caribbean and the Indian Ocean were either under dictatorships or ruled by gangsters.

Even the stable European countries had spawned a bloodthirsty generation of youth that delighted in kidnap and murder so that he, as an American diplomat, would need to be guarded night and day. He sighed. It seemed that just about everywhere touched by man had been polluted.

It seemed that all news was bad news, problems without solutions. If God really was dead, he thought, then the devil was certainly alive and kicking. He looked out into Grosvenor Square. A group of demonstrators marched in a circle, holding placards. He could not see what their particular gripe was. Every day there was some kind of protest. He could not remember a day when the square was free of it.

The older diplomats said they had seen nothing like it since the terrible days of Vietnam, but that, at least, was a concentrated protest, a demonstration against one particular situation. Now there were all manner of complaints, a generation of prophets of doom.

In the square, many were dressed in skeleton

costumes of black sacking, the bones painted a luminous white. As he gazed at them, one of the skeletons turned and seemed to look directly at him. From a distance of a hundred yards, a fist was shaken at him.

Brennan sighed and moved away from the window. He was sick of the sound of wailing and lamentation and he longed for some optimism; but deep down he knew that they all had a case. It was hard to argue with them. The world was not a place for hope, not a place, as Margaret never tired of saying, to bring babies into.

He checked his diary: cocktails with an Anglo-American trade association at the Hilton. With luck he would be home for dinner by nine.

He wandered through to the bathroom and pulled back the shower curtain, trying to force the depression from his mind, trying to think what he would say to the businessmen. At least there were to be no formal speeches, just a few words about peace through trade and the special relationship. He hoped he could sound enthusiastic.

The conference room had been decorated with American and British flags and the association's logo. For half an hour Brennan mingled, shaking hands and offering encouragement for the various ventures, his practiced eye noting the name on the lapel badge as he was introduced.

It was basically a masculine occasion, formal and restrained, but Brennan wondered idly what it would be like in a couple of hours when the cocktails had done their work and these same dignified men would be plotting mischief.

The faces and voices became an indistinct blur, until he found himself in a small oasis of space, suddenly alone. A waiter approached with a tray of drinks. Brennan took one, and as he sipped it, he was aware of someone behind him. He turned, to see a small man, nervously holding out a hand in greeting.

"Mr. Ambassador, may I have a quick word?"

Brennan placed the accent as Illinois.

"Mr. Finn," he said, shaking his hand. Unlike the others, the man did not have the name of a company beneath his name.

As if reading his mind, Finn shrugged. "I am not a member of the organization," he said apologetically. "I shouldn't really be here. A friend of a friend invited me." He saw a frown flit across Brennan's face. "It's all right," he said. "I'm sure your security people have checked me out. I'm a historian and a dealer in antiques."

"Ah," said Brennan.

"I've been trying to see you for some time, but my requests for an appointment don't seem to have filtered through your front office."

"I'm sorry, Mr. Finn, but if I were to see everyone who turned up at the—"

"Quite. I understand, but if I may have just a few seconds of your time." He took Brennan's arm and drew him into an alcove. "I have had a package delivered to your home this evening. All I ask is that you do me the courtesy of reading it."

"Of course," said Brennan, stifling a yawn.

"All I ask is that you read it through and do not dismiss it out of hand as nonsense."

Brennan frowned. He was reminded of something, a conversation he could not quite place until Finn continued.

"Much of what you will read will appear to be insane. Maybe some of it *is* insane. All I will say at this stage is that two people who have been involved in this"—he paused—"this business have died, one of them my own priest in Chicago."

"Yes, well . . ." Brennan tried to move away, but the old man held his arm.

"My priest discovered, Mr. Brennan, that the body of one of your predecessors is not in its grave."

Brennan smiled and tried to free his arm.

"Start from that fact," Finn whispered urgently. "We are talking about Damien Thorn."

Brennan pulled his arm free.

"Ask yourself why Damien Thorn's coffin contains a pile of rocks."

Brennan backed away and Finn followed him. "I am not a lunatic, Mr. Brennan. I have nothing to gain from all this. I am also a frightened man, a devout coward."

An aide, seeing Brennan's embarrassment, approached them.

"Will you do what I ask, Mr. Brennan? Just read the contents of the package all the way through."

Brennan looked down at the anxious, pleading face.

"Okay," he said. Anything to get rid of the man.

Finn smiled. "Thank you, Mr. Ambassador."
He shrugged off the attention of the aide and
moved away, smiling happily, as if a load of responsibility had been taken from his shoulders.

Chapter 9

As the massive Boeing 777 Jumbo heaved itself off
the runway at Heathrow Airport and banked
west, Michael Finn pushed himself deeper into his
seat and sighed deeply, blowing out air like a
spouting whale. He was glad to be gone, but the
relief was tinged with guilt. Maybe he could have
done more, but he doubted it. By now Philip
Brennan would know everything. He had no
doubt that he would be intrigued. Equally he had
no doubt that the man would dismiss the package
as a load of nonsense.

But once he, Michael Finn, had shown that the
body of Damien Thorn was not in its grave, then
surely Brennan would start to wonder.

He was looking forward to the notoriety. He
would start with one of the reporters on the *Chicago Tribune* who would dig away at the story
and come up with the dirt. Finn smiled at the
play on words.

He had met a few reporters and he knew how
they worked at a story. Soon they would be asking
questions all over the Thorn empire, and maybe

Thomas Doolan's dreadful death would not have been totally without some purpose.

He ordered a martini from a redheaded stewardess who introduced herself as Denise and wished him a pleasant flight. Her smile, he thought, seemed more sincere than the standard grimace of the professional. Her breast nudged his shoulder as she fixed his tray and he imagined that she winked at him. As he sipped his gin, he chuckled to himself and told himself not to be so silly—an old man weaving fantasies.

During the film she moved into the empty seat next to him and again asked if he was enjoying his flight and was there anything she could do for him?

"No," he whispered. "Everything is fine."

They watched the movie together—something about the Los Angeles Police Department—but Finn could not concentrate. Again he had the audacious notion that the contact was deliberate, just the lightest touch of their thighs, and again he cursed his imagination. Such things did not happen, or if they did, they happened to strapping young men, of whom there were plenty on the aircraft.

The film came to its climax in an explosion of gunfire. Denise leaned close to him and whispered that she had to serve coffee now.

Why not come to the galley and she'd fix him a cocktail? Then she was gone, leaving Finn to blink at the screen. Why not? Why not, indeed?

She had taken off her jacket and her cap and

leaned back against the cabin wall. She was sipping a vodka, telling him that she was not supposed to drink on duty. Occasionally she poked her head out and looked up the aisle. Candy was covering for her, she said, while she relaxed. She came from Denver. Where did he come from? What did he do? Was he in Europe on business or pleasure?

He answered as best he could, trying not to stare at her, trying to remain indifferent, gazing through a porthole and sipping his drink, as if he did this all the time.

"Do you like flying?"

"No," he said. "I'm one of those who can't understand how a piece of metal gets off the ground."

"Me too," she said, and giggled.

"I mean," he said, warming to the thought, "why do they insist on bringing the wheels up?"

"It can't fly with the wheels down, silly," she said.

"Yes, but what if they don't come down?"

She laughed and took his hand, turned and made her way through the galley, pulling him along behind her and squeezing into a tiny elevator.

"They always come down," she said. "I'll show you. This takes us to the under-floor galley . . . Here we are." She stepped out and Finn followed her, still clutching his drink, thinking back to the days when he read comics and the heroes were always pinching themselves to make sure they weren't dreaming.

She weaved between the ovens, the bar boxes

and trolleys, turned back to beckon him on, smiled as he was wedged between two trolleys, then pulled him free. He stumbled against her and she tweaked his nose, then danced away from him toward a heavy door.

He was breathless when he reached her, and as he gulped his gin, he could feel his pulse race and his heart batter against his ribs.

"The wheels are through there," she said, "in the center hold." She glanced at a light bulb that glowed red. "Once we get below pressurization level, the light goes green and we can go in."

"How long will that be?" he asked. He hoped it would be hours.

"There it goes," she said. She pushed the door open and he followed her into the center hold, shivering with the drop in temperature. He threw back the last of his drink and followed her toward a large steel container that dominated the hold.

"Come on up," she said, climbing a ladder to the top of the structure. He climbed behind her and squatted on the top.

"This is the wheel well bay," she said, pulling back a hatch. "See?"

He peered through the hatch at the massive wheels a few inches beneath.

"Sixteen," she said. "Four bogeys of four wheels each. Five feet high."

He grunted at her, half-listening as she explained how the hydraulics worked and that if they failed, which never happened, then the wheel well doors below could be opened by hand and they would simply fall out.

"Gravity, see?"

"Oh, yes." He felt cheated. When she had offered to show him the wheels, he didn't think she actually meant to show him the damned wheels.

"Any second now," she said, kneeling beside him. He heard the hiss of hydraulics as the doors in the belly of the aircraft slid open. A gust of wind fluttered his shirt and made him catch his breath.

"See, the wheels are starting to move. So you've no need to worry."

He could barely hear her over the combined roar of the engines and the wind. Looking down past the wheels, he could see the houses below, the suburbs of New York.

Again he shivered, holding on to the rim of the hatch. He began to move back, then felt her hands on his shoulders. He smiled to himself. She chose a strange time to . . . and then he was pitching forward, the wind catching in his throat, his arms flailing, grabbing at the wheel struts, his face smashing into the rubber tire, screaming in pain as one leg was jammed. He grabbed hold of the tire and looked back over his shoulder, saw her waving at him and smiling as she closed the hatch.

He slithered forward, clutching rubber, then moved no farther. His nose was pressed into a deep tread in the tire and he sniffed dung, English dung, he thought crazily, picked up from the runway on takeoff.

Whimpering, he tried to crawl back up the strut, but his leg was trapped, his body pressed hard against the metal by the slipstream, flattening him against it as if he were glued there.

He reached forward, his nails digging into rubber, scratching at the mud. Flakes peeled off and flew back into his face, lodging in one eye and causing it to water. Below, he caught a glimpse of Kennedy Airport. His wife would be there. She had traveled down especially to meet him. She was probably standing in the observation area right now, searching the sky for his flight.

He rubbed his face against the tire and remembered something Denise had said: that sometimes they hit the runway with such force that an inch of rubber was scorched off the tires.

His vision cleared and now he could see the runway ahead. Slowly and painfully he raised his head and screamed.

The small boy sitting in a window seat above the wing held his mother's hand and cried softly. A stewardess bent toward him and smiled, asking what was the matter.

"It's his first flight," said the mother.

"There it is again," said the boy, searching the stewardess's face for support.

"He says he can hear screams," said his mother apologetically. "I've told him it's only the wind."

"That's right," said the stewardess, patting his hand. "We are coming in at two hundred miles per hour. It's only the wind."

The boy shrank deeper into his seat, his ear to the window. He shut his eyes as the aircraft approached the runway, then stuck his fingers in his ears, waiting for the screaming to stop. There was a bump, the squeal of rubber against concrete, and the roar of the engines in reverse thrust, then a gentle hum as it taxied toward the terminal gate.

He did not open his eyes until the aircraft had come to a halt, and when he looked down, he saw a mechanic staring in horrified fascination at the wheels and at the mess that once was Michael Finn.

"The screaming's stopped now," he said, smiling at his mother.

Part Two

His voice, relayed through two banks of speakers, echoed around the square.

"In Bonn, in Paris, The Hague, Rome and many other cities, similar demonstratio to this

Chapter 10

Philip Brennan smiled at the two young men in the elevator and murmured a good evening. At first he paid no attention to their conversation, his mind still preoccupied with the contents of the afternoon diplomatic bag. He breathed deeply, trying to force the problems to the back of his mind, thinking of Margaret's words: that he should make use of the journey home to clear his mind so that they could share dinner together and talk about trivial things. She was right. He was in danger of becoming a workaholic.

"Can you image it? Out of a goddamn Jumbo?"

The conversation trickled through to him.

"Not good for your health, I'd say."

"They identified him from the passenger manifest, by process of elimination apparently. A Chicago man. Antique dealer or something."

Brennan turned and stared at them.

"What's that?" he asked. "Who was from Chicago?"

"Some poor guy fell out of a Jumbo as it was landing at Kennedy," said one of the young men. "It was on the news."

"Was his name Finn?"

"Yeah, that's right." The man looked at him in surprise. "Did you know him, sir?"

The elevator door opened and Brennan walked out, shaking his head, murmuring a thank-you.

The young men watched him go and followed him through the hallway.

"Strange," said one.

"He's overworked. Can't be much fun acting as a gofer between Washington and London on this Middle East business."

They shrugged at each other as they moved toward the door.

"They reckon he was squashed on impact and smeared on the wheel for two miles."

"Yeah. Messy. You want a beer?"

That evening Brennan tried to rid his mind of Michael Finn, but the man's face seemed to be printed on his brain, the thin voice pleading with him. He had no appetite and picked at his dinner, absentmindedly answering Margaret's questions and nodding as she talked about some trip she had planned.

"Charming," she said sharply, prodding him with a finger.

"Huh?"

"I'm talking to you and you're looking at your watch."

He apologized and switched on the television in time for the main news. The death of Finn was the next-to-last item, just a few seconds, almost an afterthought, the newsreader saying that Pan Am was holding an investigation into the accident.

"Poor little bastard," said Brennan.

"Probably drunk," said Margaret.

He looked at her in surprise, shocked at her callousness, but she merely smiled at him and snuggled up to him. Then it was her turn to look surprised as he roughly pushed her off and strode out of the room without a word.

Finn's package had been flung unopened among a pile of magazines in the study. He opened it, pulled out two envelopes, a sheaf of notes and a magazine article. Stapled to the first page of the notes was a single sheet of paper headed with the address of a London hotel.

"Dear Mr. Ambassador," he read. "Thank you for taking an interest. Please read the notes and the letters in the order I have indicated. I beg you to continue to the end. I will be in touch soon with some concrete evidence."

Finn's signature was neat and legible and followed by a postscript:

> The best lack all conviction, while the worst
> Are full of passionate intensity.
> Yeats, "The Second Coming"

He reached for a brandy bottle and poured himself a glass. Margaret had been saying that he was drinking too much lately, but to hell with it.

He spread the first letter on his desk.

"Next week, Father, I am due to enter a clinic. . . ." He sipped the brandy and leaned closer, moving his desk lamp so that it shone directly onto the page. When he had finished, he reached for the second letter.

"Forgive me, Father, for I have sinned . . ."

He groaned and passed his hand over his brow—not this again. He leaned back in his chair, the letter from Mary Lamont clenched in his fist. One part of him wanted to crush it and throw it away, but the grip of curiosity was stronger. He leaned forward and read through it, neatly put it back in the envelope, and picked up the sheaf of notes, neatly typed and headed "Monastery of San Benedetto."

Father De Carlo had written his notes with commendable simplicity, telling of the days eighteen years ago when a constellation of stars had come together in the region of Cassiopoiea, how he and six monks had traveled to England on a mission to destroy the Antichrist, how they had struggled with the powers of darkness, and how the six monks had given their lives.

Brennan frowned and flicked through the pages for details, but there were none. De Carlo continued his narrative, saying that the three stars, in their alignment, signaled the Second Coming of Christ and that finally the Antichrist was destroyed.

Brennan read out the last paragraph in a croaking whisper.

"I thought it was the final conflict, but I was mistaken. God guide the next man or woman, for there can be no more mistakes. The Son of God walks the earth. The spirit of the Antichrist lives. Soon they must meet in the last days."

The final letter was from Michael Finn.

"To understand," Finn had written, "you will need a Bible. . . ."

He got to his feet and moved rather unsteadily to the shelves. The Bible was dusty. He blew at it and coughed, trying to remember when he had last opened it.

Finn had written his notes clearly and Brennan had no trouble following the thesis.

"And the Lord spake unto Moses . . ." he read from Leviticus. "And ye shall hallow the fiftieth year. . . . A jubilee shall that fiftieth year be unto you."

Then: "For nation shall rise against nation. . . ." He glanced at Finn's notes. "There are those who believe that this refers to World War I. 'There shall be famines, and pestilences and earthquakes in diverse places: Matthew 24.' And indeed there were, in Italy, China, and Japan.

" 'This generation will by no means pass away until all those things occur.'

"The last days, as Matthew called them, were only the beginning," Finn had written. "The Second World War, worldwide famine, the jubilee attacks on Israel; and now there can be only a few remaining of the generation that saw the Great War. The last days are soon to come to an end as it has been prophesied, not only in the Bible but in the words of scholars such as Justin and Tertullian."

Brennan rubbed his eyes and reached for the bottle.

"The last days," he read. "The jubilee, the rise of the Antichrist, the Second Coming of Our Lord, the final battle over Israel. It is a jigsaw puzzle with a full set of pieces. Put them together and the conclusion is inescapable: the picture on the box of the jigsaw shows Armageddon, the final battle between good and evil, fought over Israel.

"May we pray that the rest of the prophecy comes true and that the final battle will be followed by the Millennium, a thousand years of peace."

Brennan pushed the letter aside. "But what kind of peace?" he said aloud. "The peace of the dead, the peace of a dead planet?"

He shook his head to clear it, reached for the bottle, and discovered that he had drunk a third of it, yet he did not remember refilling his glass.

The last document was a copy of Carol Wyatt's article. He squinted at it, but was no longer in the mood to read any further.

"Madness," he croaked. He rose to his feet, snapped off the lamp, and made for the door, stumbling slightly. He hoped that Margaret would be asleep. For the first time in his marriage he did not want to hear her voice, nor feel her insistent fingers upon him.

Quietly he slipped in beside her. She was breathing deeply and scarcely stirred. For a moment he gazed through the open window at the night sky, idly trying to put a name to the combination of stars, then gave up, closed his eyes, and fell instantly asleep.

He stood beside the font, Margaret at his side holding the baby. A choir sang and an organ blasted out a psalm, the sound deafening him. He leaned across and kissed his wife on the cheek. He was proud of her. She had never wanted to bring a child into the world, but she had done it, against her better judgment. He looked down at the baby, wrapped in a shawl. It smiled at him, toothless grin, and held out pudgy arms. He tickled its palm and the tiny hand grasped his finger and held on.

The voice of the bishop cut through the sound of the singing. It was a familiar voice, thin and pleading. He frowned, trying to recollect where he had heard it before; then he remembered it as an Illinois accent. He turned and gazed at Michael Finn, who was holding out his arms for the baby.

"No." The word boomed from him and he tried to stop Margaret handing over the baby, but he could not move. Finn dipped his hand in the font.

"No." Again he roared, but no one paid any attention to him. He grabbed the child, struggling with Margaret. The shawl slipped from the baby's body and he could see the thick greasy animal hair on its shoulders. The baby chuckled and looked up at him. Obscenities flowed from its mouth and he was aware of a foul stench in the cathedral. Finn took his hand from the font and smeared the child's head with offal. Again it laughed, gripping his hand. The choir sang and

119

he dragged his eyes away from the child, gazing at the domed roof, trying to free himself from its grip.

"Yea, though I have walked through the valley of the shadow of death, I will fear no evil," he shouted.

And now the little fingers were gouging at his eyes and he could hear Margaret laugh, her voice insistent: "What's wrong? Let him play." And he wanted to run, but his legs would not move. He closed his eyes tighter and bawled out the words, trying to raise his voice above the chorus of laughter. . . .

His eyes snapped open.

"Thy rod and thy staff they comfort me. . . ." His voice boomed through the bedroom. He was sitting up, his hands at his eyes, clawing at them. He peered between his fingers and saw Margaret staring at him, gripping the sheet with one hand, the other at her mouth, her eyes wide and terrified, staring back at him as if he were mad.

He shook his head, trying to clear away the remnants of his dream, then reached out for her, but she backed away from him, and still he could hear his voice, although he was not conscious of speaking.

"Thou anointest my head with oil; my cup runneth over."

Margaret slid from the bed, still clutching the sheet, and backed against the curtains. For a moment he lay watching her, then ran naked for the bathroom, trying to escape the stench that pervaded the room. He slammed the door behind him and leaned against it and still his lips moved:

"Surely goodness and mercy shall follow me all the days of my life: and I will dwell in the house of the Lord for ever."

He sighed and blew out bad breath, rubbed his face with his left hand. His chin felt soft and smooth and round. He ran his hand over his head and he felt it pulse and throb as if the skull had not joined, and when he looked in the mirror, the face of the newborn baby grinned back at him, a child covered in thick hair, its mouth dribbling vomit.

That morning he was at his desk early. He had a speech to prepare, but he could not concentrate on it. The harder he tried to push aside the memory of his nightmare, the more it intruded upon his thoughts.

All morning he went through the motions of working, making phone calls that made little sense, and snapping at his secretary. Lunch was a snack with a young diplomat from the Foreign Office. They talked about the upcoming meeting and he hoped that he had been articulate, but as he left the table, he realized that there were gaps in his memory and he noticed the young man shoot him a brief glance of anxiety as they shook hands.

Back at his desk he thought again about the package he had locked away in his study and a name jumped to the front of his mind. He tapped the intercom.

"Get me Jim Gregory."

A moment later the chief press attaché's voice crackled through the machine.

"Jim, did we get an interview request from a reporter called Carol Wyatt? Quite recently, I think."

"Just a moment, sir." There was a pause while the man checked his files. "Yes, sir," he said. "A strange request, about daggers or something."

"Tell her I'll see her."

"But, sir, she's way down the list. I mean, she's a nobody and the subject matter is—"

"Just get her."

"As you wish."

Brennan leaned back and looked up at the Great Seal, winked at the eagle.

"He thinks I'm cracking up," he said, to the bird and to himself. He paced the office. Outside, the protesters circled the square. He stared at them unblinking, then twitched, startled, as the intercom buzzed.

"Gregory, sir. It seems your reporter has vanished. She hasn't been seen since the day she sent in her request."

"Oh, Christ." Brennan slumped into his chair.

"Anything wrong, sir?"

"No, it's okay."

"Do you want me to keep the interview on file for when she turns up?"

"Yes, but I don't think . . ." His voice trailed away.

"Sir?"

"Yes. Keep her on file."

Another one, he thought, counting on his fingers: Reynolds, Lamont, De Carlo, Finn, Doolan, and now Wyatt, all dead, missing, or mad.

The priest was the only one who was definitely alive, and he was insane. Or was he? The idea that the priest might not be mad was, in itself, a crazy idea; for if he were not mad, then the idea did not bear thinking about.

Again the intercom buzzed. His secretary telling him that she knew he did not want any calls but Washington was on the line. It was the State Department.

Brennan picked up the phone and mumbled a hello. It was Bill Jeffries, an old friend. They had been at college together, and now Bill was practically running the State Department. He was calling to talk about the Foreign Secretary's meeting.

"You'll keep your ears open, of course." Jeffries said.

"That's what I'm paid for."

"Oh, and, Philip, I see you have a vacation scheduled for next month. I'm sorry, but it looks like you're going to have to postpone it. It's a bad time."

"Yeah, sure."

"Maybe in the fall."

"Sure." He was about to hang up when a thought crossed his mind. Jeffries was a good man, a discreet man. He would not be fazed by his request.

"Bill, how do we go about getting an official exhumation?"

"Depends who it is."

"Damien Thorn."

"What? What's the matter with you, Philip?"

"Is there any way of checking that the body of Thorn is in his grave?"

"Jesus, Philip."

"I know. It sounds crazy. But can it be done?"

"I don't know."

"Can you find out the procedure? Discreetly?"

"Yes, I suppose so. But why?"

"If I told you, you'd have me committed."

They laughed together, the old college friends, and when Brennan hung up, he felt better, as if he had shared some of the burden.

In Washington, Jeffries called to his secretary: "Get me the Thorn Corporation. Right away."

Chapter 11

Paul Buher was becoming concerned about himself. Lately his mind had been producing images of cabins by the lakes, fishing poles and rocking chairs, a bottle of bourbon by a log fire, and vacations. As hard as he tried, he could not rid himself of the idea of a few days' rest. He had not had a vacation in all his adult life. Vacations were dangerous. People had gone on vacation and returned to find a space where their desks had been. When he was younger, he had occasionally made use of other people's vacations. Yet now there was this creeping desire for peace and quiet.

He cast the thought aside and put it down to jet lag, yet another Atlantic crossing. But it was more than that. Last night he had seriously played with the notion of staying in Chicago; he had no need to be in London for the conference, the delegates could easily have reported to him by telephone. It had taken him an hour to convince himself to make the trip. There was no doubt about it. He was slowing up.

It was almost midnight by the time the limousine reached Pereford. George, as ever, was waiting by the front door, smiling a welcome.

"How are you, George?" He handed over his coat.

"Very well, sir," the butler replied, but there was a look of concern that he could not conceal.

"You sure?"

"Quite sure, sir." George colored slightly and led him to the drawing room. "He will be down directly, sir."

"He's awake, then?"

"Yes, and he would like to see you."

Buher watched the butler leave the room. *Directly*, he thought, a fine old-fashioned word, but then, George was a fine old-fashioned English butler, elderly but still sprightly. *Still* sprightly. Would Paul Buher still be sprightly at that age? he asked himself.

He spread himself on the sofa and closed his eyes. When he opened them again, the boy was standing beside him, staring at him curiously.

"You look exhausted," the boy said.

"Age, my friend, defeats us all eventually."

"Mmm." The sound was noncommittal. "Are you too tired to tell me about the meeting?"

"Of course not." Buher sat up, reached for his briefcase, and flipped a report sheet at the boy. He studied it and looked up.

"So," he said, "Simon will block anything the others come up with."

Buher nodded.

"Then the meeting will adjourn?"

"Yes."

"But this merely leaves us with the status quo." The tone was irritable.

"Well?" Buher looked puzzled. "This is what we want. It has always been our strategy. Divide and rule. Turn chaos into stalemate and back again to controlled chaos. In such a way we keep our position as—"

"But this is not progress," the boy said sharply.

"Progress toward what?" asked Buher in exasperation.

"Toward destruction." The boy flipped the paper back into Buher's face, turned, and walked out of the room.

Buher watched him go and sighed, thinking reluctantly of the old days. The boy's father had never talked in riddles. You could work with him.

He awoke early, his sleep disturbed by forgotten dreams. As he showered and dressed, he tried to avoid the sight of his reflection. It was an old face now and a sagging body. The sleep had not refreshed him. His eyes felt sticky and his breath was foul. He spat into the basin and left the room, swallowing a yawn.

As he passed the boy's room, he tapped on the door. There was no sound, not even the predictable snuffling of the dog. He opened the door and peered inside. The bed had been slept in. The sheets were twisted, the pillow on the floor. He was about to close the door when he caught sight of the montage. He squinted. It was somehow different. He stepped inside and peered at it. Next to the print of Kate Reynolds' tombstone was a

127

series of color pictures. The first showed a young woman lying naked in the black chapel, the large brown eyes gazing upward with the blank stare of the dead. Next to it, a second picture showed the body in the first stage of decomposition. Then another, and a fourth.

Buher leaned, trembling, against the wall. His hand fluttered across the photographs, dislodging one and sending it fluttering to the floor; then he stumbled from the room, swallowing hard, fighting the nausea. He closed the door and moved along the corridor, struggling to compose himself. At the chapel door, the dog looked up at him and moved to one side. He tapped again. His hands were clammy and he wondered if he could bear to see whatever was inside. But he had to go in. He needed to know what was going on. There was no sound. Slowly he pushed the door open and stepped inside. It took him a moment to focus and he stared into the face of the boy, a demented face, eyes staring back wildly at him, the hands gripping those of his father. Sweat ran down his face.

Buher surreptitiously glanced around the room, holding his breath, but there was nothing new in the place, no obscene additions.

"Paul." The boy's voice startled him, a barking noise.

Buher obediently stepped back into the doorway.

"Leave me."

He did as he was told, backing away and closing the door, glad to be gone.

In the drawing room he poured himself a drink and rang for the butler. The old man looked in, his head cocked to one side, like a spaniel.

"Do you know anything about a visitor? A young woman?"

Again the old man looked worried. "Only that there was a car, sir. The young master instructed me to get someone to drive it away and lose it. I do believe it belonged to a young woman."

"Why did you not tell me? You know that you are to report anything unusual."

"He told me not to mention it, sir. He would have known if I disobeyed him." He paused and shrugged. "He will know by now that I have told you. There are no secrets."

Buher nodded and waved his hand in a gesture of dismissal. George hesitated. "I hope he is not angry." He smiled at Buher. "I have not long to live and I have always been faithful. I hope that he does not condemn me to an eternity of sanctimony."

Buher smiled back. "No. He cannot do that. It is the one power that is beyond him. Your soul is safely damned, old man."

"Yes," said George. "I suppose so."

As Buher waited for the boy, he gazed out at the lawns and beyond to the woods. The place was calm. Nothing moved. There was no wind. He wanted to be out there, on his own, away from the house. He did not hear the boy come in, and turned, startled, at the sound of his name. The boy had composed himself but his face was gray with fatigue.

"Are you ill?" Buher asked.

The boy shook his head. "It is Him. I feel Him everywhere. His influence. His blessed power." He slumped into a chair and sighed. Buher moved toward him, feeling curiously protective. The boy, after all, had not chosen his destiny; but as he reached out to comfort him, he remembered something he had to tell him.

"We have a slight problem."

The boy looked up at him.

"You've heard me talk about Philip Brennan."

The boy looked away and sniffed.

"It seems that he—"

"It's all right, Paul," said the boy dismissively.

Buher looked at him inquiringly.

"He will destroy himself," the boy said in a matter-of-fact tone.

Buher nodded. He should have realized. Whenever there was any danger to him, the boy knew, and he acted accordingly. The feeling of protectiveness had been misplaced.

Which reminded him . . .

"Who was the woman?" he asked. "The pictures on your wall?"

The boy shrugged. "He sent her. She was like a fawn."

"Christ," said Buher.

"Don't blaspheme," the boy snapped at him.

"And what about the body? The remains?"

"I disposed of them," said the boy, smiling. "Such a task is, after all, in my blood."

Buher's hands clenched into claws. He stood over the boy, glaring at him. "It is an outrage," he said. "It's a . . ." He searched for the word. ". . . an indignity. Your father would never have stooped so low, to soil his hands in such a manner." Buher's face reddened in anger. "Your father—"

The boy jumped to his feet. "Be quiet," he snapped, pushing Buher so that he stumbled and fell onto the sofa. "Do not talk to me about my father."

"He would never have done such a thing," Buher persisted. "Everything was done for a reason. There was a method. You talk of destruction, but your father talked of control. Everything was done so that he might get control of the world and of men's souls . . ."

"What?" the boy snarled at him. "Do you have the arrogance to think he cared about your petty souls? Do you think he had any interest in your miserable souls?"

Buher ripped a ring from his finger and held his hand in front of the boy's face, pointing to the cluster of sixes.

" 'And he causeth all, both small and great, rich and poor, free and bond, to receive a mark in their right hand, or in their foreheads: And that no man might buy or sell, save he that had the mark.' " He got to his feet and stood his full height. "Revelation," he said. "Buy or sell. Control. That is what we have worked for so that he might—"

"Pap," the boy spat the word at him, spraying him with saliva. "Do not quote to me. You are a dupe, like the rest of them. When the angel was

cast out, there was only one inevitable consequence, and that is destruction, sweet vengeance."
He smiled. "Vengeance is mine!"

Buher stood motionless as the boy walked
around him, prodding him, taunting him.

"Two thousand years, my father said, have been
enough. You talk of control, your philosophers
prattle about freedom of choice, the free will to
choose between my father and the Nazarene.
Well, Paul, there is one freedom left. You, with
your machinations between survival and total
destruction, have helped man choose. You have
helped lead mankind by the nose toward the
abyss." He pinched Buher's face. "One tweak, and
he is gone. . . ." He smiled, turned, and left
the room; Buher could hear him laughing as he
called out to the dog.

Buher waited until the footsteps had died away,
then moved into the hall, slowly climbed the staircase, and stopped outside the boy's room. He
could hear him moving around and he could
smell the dog. Holding his breath, he tiptoed
along the corridor toward the chapel and quietly
entered. For a moment he stood motionless, then
moved toward the corpse. He knelt, reached for
the hand, and grasped it. The fingers reminded
him of his schooldays, of the plasticene they had
played with.

"Damien," he whispered, "ever since I was
called, I have worked toward the coming of your
father's kingdom. I have rejoiced at the prospect
of his inevitable victory. I have been faithful."

He caressed the fingers. "When your physical

life was extinguished, I prayed to your spirit and you answered me. You told me not to despair, that your time was not yet come. You answered my prayers, asking me to believe in your resurrection, that I would sit at your left hand.

"Tell me again. All we have done. It is control, Damien, not destruction?"

He bowed and knelt in silence, as if awaiting instructions, then snapped his head up as a shaft of light illuminated Damien's face and his eyes appeared to come alive. He blinked, then was aware of the sound of suppressed snarling. He turned. The light came from the doorway, where the boy and the dog stood, staring at him.

"What are you doing?" The boy's voice was flat and emotionless.

"Seeking guidance."

"Then seek it elsewhere. Leave me with my father."

Buher got to his feet, his knees crackling. The boy stood to one side to let him pass, and slowly Buher wandered back the way he had come, feeling confused, defeated, and very old.

Chapter 12

They came to the rally in hundreds of thousands.
London was jammed from the City in the east to
Sloane Square in the west. Nothing moved from
Oxford Street south to the Embankment and at
the center of it all, in Trafalgar Square, the police
and the press gave up trying to estimate the
crowds and gave out the first number that came
into their heads.

There was not the carnival atmosphere of previous Campaign for Nuclear Disarmament marches.
No musicians played; no theater groups entertained. It was all too serious for that. The crowd
moved in toward the square, becoming denser every minute, and the police, on foot and on
horseback, watched in silence.

The first speech was due to be given at two
P.M., and at one-thirty, Paul Buher's limousine
came to a halt in Pimlico. In the back, he and the
boy gazed at the people moving past them in one
direction. Many were dressed in skeleton costumes,
others in shrouds. A baby in a pram had been
made up to look as if it had been hideously

134

burned. The boy grinned and chuckled, and from the floor the dog raised its head and grunted at him.

Buher pressed a button in a console that was set into the door and spoke into a grille.

"What's the problem?"

The driver's voice echoed into the back. "Jammed solid, sir. The police radio says there's no movement from here on in."

"Damn," said Buher. Silently he asked himself why the boy had insisted on coming to the rally. It was unlike him. Normally he was not afflicted with curiosity.

"We'll walk," the boy said.

"But it's a long way," Buher objected.

The boy said nothing, opened the door, and stepped out into the crowd. The dog padded after him; Buher, sighing, left instructions with the driver where he could pick them up, and followed him. They walked at the same pace as the crowd. A German shepherd, trotting ahead of them, turned, gazed at the boy and the dog, and loped off down a side street, its ears flat against its head.

It was a humid day and the crowd perspired. The boy's nostrils twitched and he kept his hand lightly on the dog's head. Buher moved behind them, glancing now and again at his watch. The meeting in Whitehall would be into the plenary session by now and his staff would be reporting to headquarters within the hour. He should have been in his office. There was no need for this nonsense. He grunted as a youth carrying a banner bumped him.

"Watch where you're going," he snapped, and the young man backed off, wide-eyed, hurt, innocent, confused by the hostility. Weren't they all of the same mind, marching together to save the world?

"Fool," Buher grunted. He felt nothing but contempt for them all: naive, blinkered, sheeplike, fools who knew nothing of the realities of the world. Grimly he followed the boy into Victoria, along the Mall, and toward Trafalgar Square. Now they could hear the crackle of the loudspeakers and the roar of the crowd, the crashing waves of applause punctuated by the whirr of police helicopters.

As they reached the square, the crowd was motionless and densely packed, but the boy and the dog forced their way through, Buher keeping tightly behind them. There were grunts of annoyance as they shoved forward, complaints that were soon stifled by the sight of the dog. One man who would not move was butted by the great head, and when he looked down to object, the dog snarled at him. They reached the foot of Nelson's Column and made a space for themselves against one of the stone lions, looking across at the platform ten yards away, built up twenty feet from the ground. Two closed circuit television screens had been erected on either side of the platform, fifteen feet high, showing close-ups of the young speaker, a Tribunite politician, popular with the crowd, the grandson of one of the founders of the movement.

His voice, relayed through two banks of speakers, echoed around the square.

"In Bonn, in Paris, The Hague, Rome, and many other cities, similar demonstrations to this one are taking place simultaneously."

The crowd roared its approval at the clumsy phrase.

"In five hours' time, there will be a march on Washington. Tomorrow will be the turn of the Far East and Australia. Our friends in Moscow, Prague, Budapest, and Warsaw will learn of our efforts and gain strength for their struggle. . . ."

Buher yawned.

"And now," said the young politician, "James Graham."

The noise battered the eardrums. Buher put his hands to his head and looked up at the boy who had clambered onto the base of the column. He was looking around, seemingly searching for someone; then his eyes fixed on a tall thin figure, white-haired, walking onto the platform, led by a golden Labrador. The dog moved toward the microphone as if pulled by a string, then sat and looked up at the old man, nudged his hand toward the stem of the mike, then calmly sat, its work done for the moment. The man raised both hands, the leash dangling from his left wrist.

Buher glanced around the crowd. They were clapping and shouting, some whistling, and he was reminded of Damien Thorn's effect on his followers, except that they were more honest. Would these people die for James Graham? he asked himself. What was more, would they kill for him? He doubted it.

The screens brought the old man's face into sharp focus, a gnarled, blind face, the dark glasses reflecting the flashing of cameras. He had been described as the most natural successor to Bertrand Russell. He was a philosopher and a humanist, wiser than the politicians, with a gift for oratory that could bring together the intellectuals and the workers.

Again Buher looked up at the boy. He was staring at Graham, ignoring the screens, ignoring the crowd, his gaze fixed on the old man's face. Buher felt something move and looked down at the dog between him and the boy. Its front paws rested on the plinth and it too stared at the platform as if hypnotized.

Graham lowered his hands and the noise ceased abruptly, as if someone had hit a switch. He cleared his throat and the noise was like thunder. The guide dog's ears pricked and it looked up at him as if to check that he was all right.

"Friends." His voice was deep and strong. "I have been told that this is the biggest demonstration ever seen in this city."

A tremble of noise began, but he quelled it instantly by raising one hand.

"A very great man, a journalist called James Cameron, one of the founders of our movement, once said of an organization with a similar aim to ours. 'I wish,' he said. 'I wish to God that Oxfam did not exist.' " He paused. "I echo him. I wish to God that the Campaign for Nuclear Disarmament did not exist, had no need to exist."

This time the applause rose unchecked and he gazed sightlessly to right and left.

Again he raised one hand. Again there was silence.

"This afternoon, less than a mile from here, men are meeting in an attempt to do something about a crisis that has existed in varying degrees for over fifty years, that has threatened that part of the globe we know as the Middle East, and that, by extension, threatens us all. We wish the politicians wisdom and determination, but such a wish is not enough. What I demand from them and what I demand from you, the voters, is simplicity itself. It is what I have always demanded. That you choose only those men and women who run for office under our banner. . . ." A roar of approval. "That you forget the irrelevance of party politics . . ." Another roar. "That you, each one of you, act single-mindedly for the salvation of humanity by focusing solely on the survival of our species."

For a full minute the square echoed to the cheers of the crowd. To his left, Buher noticed a group of policemen staring at the platform and clapping along with the others. He shook his head, wondering for the thousandth time how people could put up with platitudes in place of realities.

"What political debate has any meaning in a wasteland?" Graham demanded.

"None," roared the crowd, as if rehearsed.

"What value is there in discussing alternative forms of society in a planet reduced to rubble?"

Again: "None."

The old man held up both hands, and the dog, noticing the tug on the leash, got to its feet.

"As many of you will know," said Graham, "I am not a religious man. Nonetheless, I will quote you Paul's second epistle to Timothy." He cleared his throat and the dog gazed out over the crowd, scraping at the platform floor with one paw.

Buher noticed that the boy had shifted his gaze to the guide dog, staring unblinking at it.

" 'This know also,' " said Graham, " 'that in the last days perilous times shall come. For men shall be lovers of their own selves, covetous, boasters, proud, blasphemers, disobedient to parents, unthankful, unholy, without natural affection, trucebreakers, false accusers, incontinent, fierce, despisers of those that are good, traitors, heady, highminded, lovers of pleasures more than lovers of God.' "

The guide dog rose onto its hind legs, its front paws crisscrossing across its face, then dropped to a stance once more, head bobbing, sniffing the air. To Buher, it seemed as if it were now looking directly at the boy on the column.

"I call for you who have faith to pray to your gods," said Graham. "And those without faith to look to your intellects."

The boy concentrated his gaze on the guide dog

as the screens switched to long shot and the dog could be seen by the crowd, pawing the platform, its hackles rising, a dribble of saliva hanging from its muzzle.

"My theme," continued the old man, "is not new. But the present situation makes it all the more—"

The dog leaped at him, jaws snapping at his master's face. He stumbled backward, the cord of the microphone curling around his leg, and as he fell, his amplified scream echoed around the square. No one moved. The stewards at the side of the platform stood momentarily transfixed, unable to react.

The dog moved back, allowing the old man to scramble unsteadily to his feet, the leash still wrapped around his wrist.

"Oh, my God," he breathed, and the whisper hissed around the square. He put one hand to his face and those near enough could see the blood trickle between his fingers. The television director, acting instinctively, brought the cameras into close-up, and the crowd gasped as Graham's torn face filled the screens. His glasses hung over one ear and his bloodied fingers clawed at the empty sockets. The stewards were running toward him now; the dog turned to look at them, then gazed out over the crowd and leaped toward the edge of the platform, dragging the old man behind him.

Someone, one lone woman, screamed in anticipation as the dog hurled itself into space and Graham grabbed at air, vainly and blindly searching for a hold, before toppling off the platform. The cameras followed him down, the microphone picking up his scream, the sound system functioning perfectly, catching the crunch as the dog hit the concrete twenty feet below, the old man's scream dying in his throat as his skull cracked, then picking up the screams of those who rushed to him, the babble of shocked voices echoing among the crowd, which stood in shocked silence. The cord of the microphone dangled from the platform like a black umbilical cord.

The boy was the first to react. He turned and gazed at a chestnut police horse standing thirty yards away, the biggest of a wedge of ten police horses separating two sections of the crowd and keeping a clear passage through to Whitehall. The animal's head turned, causing its rider to squirm in his saddle and frown. The policeman tugged at the reins but still the horse stared wide-eyed at the boy. Its nostrils flared and the lips fluttered, showing his teeth, whinnying softly so that the others turned toward it, then followed its gaze in the direction of the boy on the column.

For a moment the big horse stood motionless, only its eyes widening in panic, then it reared, tossed its head, and bolted, taking the others with it. Three policemen were unseated by the sudden change, but the others clung on, hauling at the reins, the horses' heads jerking back but not enough to stop their momentum. A young couple, their arms linked and carrying a banner, were the first casualties, going down under the hooves of the chestnut, their screams pitiful squeaks punctuating the amplified voices of the men and women around the body of James Graham.

The riderless horses smashed farther into the crowd; others, scenting the fear and the smell of death, went berserk. Pressing himself against the column, Buher saw a riderless horse gallop toward him, men and women going down under it; then it stopped, turned, and leaped a barrier, like a steeplechaser, coming down among a group of youths, the forelegs snapping like the sound of gunfire.

The first charge of the horses had the effect of a stone thrown into water, the ripples of confusion spreading outward throughout the square as men and women fought one another to escape. Buher saw another horse throw its rider and felt a hand on his shoulder. He looked up as the boy pulled him back and clung on to him, his eyes bright; he was licking his lips.

There was chaos and still the cameras were at work, the giant screens presenting the pictures to those caught below. Buher saw a young woman try to scramble clear, holding her child high, gazing around her, searching for somewhere safe to put it before she went down with the others, her screams mingling with those of countless others.

Again he turned as he heard the boy mutter.

"Mere anarchy is loosed upon the world."

Buher shivered and pressed himself back against the stonework. The screams reached a crescendo, then abruptly died. As if someone had frozen the frame on a screen, the movement ceased. At the southeast corner of the square, the barriers leading to the safety of Whitehall had broken and the crowd had rushed through to safety, leaving room for those behind them to spread out and keep clear of the bucking horses.

Now there was room to breathe. Men, women, and children stumbled, mumbling, staring in shock at the carnage. Buher stepped out from beneath the column and gazed around him. A police horse lay dead a few yards from him, its rider crushed beneath it, one arm raised as if in salute. A pile of bodies lay in an untidy heap against the plinth of one of the stone lions, the heap convulsing like one great composite animal. The screams had changed tone to the moans of the injured and the dying. Ambulancemen with stretchers began to move among them, followed by news photographers swooping like scavengers.

One young man lay motionless, crushed by a horse. He was dressed in a skeleton costume and his bones stuck out at grotesque angles through the material. A solitary horse picked its way daintily among the bodies, hooves lifted high, as if walking through a field of daffodils, while others stood motionless, only their heads bobbing, lips twitching.

The boy jumped to the ground and took Buher's arm.

"Where are we meeting the car?"

Buher shook his head. He could not remember.

The boy stood for a moment beside a pile of

bodies, the dog next to him sniffing the air, then turned and looked at Buher.

"Blessed are the peacemakers," he said.

"Amen," Buher said, and together they pushed their way through the silent crowd.

Chapter 13

The death of James Graham shook Brennan. He heard about it during the afternoon. The first casualty figures listed thirty-eight dead and over a hundred injured. The statistics were appalling, but he found it difficult to evoke an emotional response to them, just a feeling of disgust that such a thing could happen.

With Graham, the shock was real. Since his student days. Brennan had admired the man, and the admiration had increased with the years. There were many who criticized him. Career politicians and professional cynics argued that the old man was nothing more than a bleeding-heart liberal, out of touch with reality, but Brennan knew better. He had met him twice and seen him disarm his interrogators with his sense of humor and his knowledge of world politics. There had been attempts to discredit him, crude campaigns to show him up as a Soviet tool, but not even that well-trusted ploy worked.

To Philip Brennan, James Graham was the nearest human being to a saint he had come across, and a humorous saint at that. And now he was dead, a victim of yet another accident.

He had called Margaret and asked her to video-tape the main news bulletin for him, saying he would be home late. She met him at the door as he climbed out of the car.

"You look bushed," she said.

"Bushed? Now there's a word."

She was dressed in jeans and a T-shirt, her girl-next-door look, as she called it, which made the theatrical makeup seem incongruous. They kissed in the hallway and he held her tightly, feeling the warmth of her. She moved against him, but this was not what he wanted. He needed some kind of sexless comfort. Gently he pushed her away and turned his head so that he could not see her expression of rejection.

"You saw the news?" he asked.

"Yes. Those poor horses."

He turned and gazed at her in astonishment.

"Poor things, driven mad by something—"

"Christ, Margaret . . ."

She shrugged at him and moved toward the kitchen. "I'll bring you a beer before dinner," she shouted over her shoulder.

He watched her go, then went to his study and switched on the news. It had been extended to give maximum coverage of the tragedy.

He watched as the scene flashed in front of him, winced as the dog went for Graham's face, and he involuntarily closed his eyes as the old man was dragged off the platform.

As the horses began to bolt, a newscaster, in voice-over, said that it was the first time in the history of the Metropolitan Police that such a thing had happened. The horses were trained not to bat an eyelash at anything, and an investigation was under way.

He watched and listened for twenty minutes, then ran the program through again. As the camera scanned the crowd, he blinked and froze the frame, tapped a button and focused on one section by the column, tapped another and brought the required section into close-up.

He leaned forward and stared at the screen. What on earth was Paul Buher doing at the rally? What possible interest could it hold for a man like that?

He ran the tape again and stopped it as a boy leaped off the plinth and took Buher's arm. Again he froze the frame and sat back. Almost as he began to wonder where he had seen the face, he realized who it reminded him of . . . It was the face of Damien Thorn, only fifteen or so years younger than the portrait in the embassy.

"Oh, God," he murmured.

"What are you doing?" Margaret's voice was sharp with curiosity as she handed him his beer. He snapped off the screen and looked up at her. He could not tell her.

"Just scratching an itch, that's all," he said, smiling. He could not tell her, for she would think he was insane. He could not tell someone who worried only about the horses.

The afternoon sun slanted through the blinds of the Foreign Office building, shredding the cigar smoke around the big mahogany table. For an hour the delegates had made and listened to speeches. The subject on the agenda was a recurring problem: the ownership of the Golan Heights, currently in the hands of a United Nations peacekeeping force.

Peter Stevenson was smiling, working hard to remain calm in the face of intransigence.

"Gentlemen, gentlemen," he murmured, lightly tapping his fingers on the table as two Syrian delegates spoke in chorus, their voices raised in anger, while three men from the Knesset gazed on impassively.

"Gentlemen, please."

There was a pause. The Arabs seemed to have run out of breath. Into the pause, a deep voice intruded.

"Do you not think," said Philip Brennan, "that it is about time we considered the proposal in an adult fashion instead of squabbling like so many kids in a schoolyard?"

Each face turned to him, registering various shades of surprise, those who needed translation looking inquisitive. The two Syrians got to their feet and roared at Brennan.

"Gentlemen, please." Stevenson's voice was hoarse with exasperation. He called for silence but went unheeded. One of the Israelis joined in, shouting from his seat.

Eventually Stevenson reached for a gavel and banged it hard on the table.

"The meeting is adjourned for half an hour," he said, rising to his feet, collecting his papers, and leaving the room with a quick glance of annoyance at Brennan, which a few noticed. It was unheard of for an observer to intrude.

In the corridor, two members of the British delegation raised eyebrows and murmured stage whispers.

"Does he drink, the chap?"

"Shouldn't wonder."

Brennan, moving behind them, was tempted to bang their heads together, but resisted and moved toward the coffee machine. He was filling his cup when one of the Israelis moved behind him, a small man named Simon, known in diplomatic circles to be devious and powerful.

"A timely intervention, Mr. Brennan," he said, smiling.

"I don't know what came over me," Brennan said, grinning.

Simon shrugged. "I'm sure we are pleased to have a break." He drew Brennan back against the wall. "I was talking to Paul Buher today. He tells me you were trying to reach him last night."

Brennan nodded.

"He asked me to say that he was sorry he did not return your call, but if you would like to take a drink with him this evening, about seven maybe, at his office?"

"Thanks for the message," said Brennan. Simon smiled and left him, and Brennan watched him go, wondering idly why the little man should be acting as a messenger for Buher.

"Philip, glad you could make it."

Buher's handshake was firm, but Brennan thought he could detect a strain in his expression, an unhealthy pallor lurking beneath the permanent suntan.

After a drink was poured and the preliminaries of small talk, Buher apologized for not answering his call last night.

"It was nothing," Brennan said, smiling, trying to make light of it. "I'd just seen you on television and called to commiserate."

A brief frown of incomprehension creased Buher's face.

"Just to say it must have been dreadful to actually have been present at such a horrible business."

"That was all you called about?"

Brennan nodded. "Just spur of the moment." He glanced at his glass. "Hardly worth wasting your whiskey on . . ."

Buher smiled. "Oh, you're welcome anytime."

Again they talked of nothing, inconsequential chitchat concerning the Stevenson meeting, as it had come to be known. Buher pointed to his glass, but Brennan declined, saying he had to get home.

At the door he turned. "Who was the boy you were with, Paul?"

And Buher frowned. "What boy?"

"On television, you seemed to be talking to a boy?"

Buher shrugged again. "Oh, I don't know. Just a kid I suppose. In such a crush . . . you know how it is."

"Yes, well, thanks for the drink."

He left the building still unconvinced, and on his way home he asked himself questions and got no proper answers. He had certainly been acting strangely. His interruption at the meeting was uncharactertistic, and it would certainly have been noted. The report would say: Brennan, good organizer, a fine analytical brain, but prone to lapses of self-control. If he had been asked to defend his action, he would have been in trouble. It was a small thing, but in diplomacy minor actions could lead to major incidents.

Unlike many of his friends and colleagues, he did not lean toward self-analysis. He was simply not all that interested in himself, but lately he had noticed signs of instability; there were occasional acts of irrational anger and moments of forgetfulness. And there was physical evidence: smudges under the eyes and the ever-present lethargy dragging at his eyelids. Margaret, if she had noticed, had not said anything, nor was it the function of his staff to point it out, but neither his wife nor his colleagues were fools. They must have noticed and be wondering . . .

Back home, he went straight to his study and switched on the television set. It was still tuned to the Trafalgar Square disaster. He worked the buttons, played the tape backward and forward until he was satisfied of two things: the boy was the living image of Damien Thorn, and Buher had lied when he said he did not know him.

It was a puzzle. He reached for the brandy bottle, thinking that it was just as well he had not done as he intended. He had not asked Buher about Damien Thorn's burial. At least he had not given himself away on that score.

Chapter 14

Bill Harris, chief press officer at the BBC, was flattered and intrigued by the invitation to the American embassy. In the cab taking him to Grosvenor Square, he fingered the cassette in his pocket and wondered why Brennan was interested. As he was taken up to the ambassador's office, he recalled the story of one of Brennan's predecessors, a man named Doyle, who had called a press conference, only for the reporters to find him blowing his brains out as they were summoned to his office. Harris had been a young reporter in those days and he remembered chasing around with the others, looking for a motive for Doyle's suicide and finding none.

"The ambassador will see you now."

He smiled at the secretary and walked in. Brennan held out a hand in greeting and Harris glanced past him at the Great Seal of the United States, on which Doyle's brains had been spattered by the bullet. He remembered seeing the photograph, which was so obscene that it had never been published but which had circulated among the photographers.

"Nice of you to come," said Brennan.

"We're always glad to be of assistance."

"You've brought the tape?"

Harris took it from his pocket and Brennan pointed toward a television set and poured coffee while Harris inserted the cassette.

They settled down to watch, sipping their coffee as the screen filled with the program title: *World in Focus.*

A woman smiled at the camera and began her introduction.

"Kate was a beautiful woman," said Harris softly. "And talented."

"You knew her?"

"Vaguely. It was tragic. She was so young."

"Are you a religious man, Mr. Harris?"

Harris blinked at the unexpected remark. "I'm afraid not."

"She died of cancer, I understand," said Brennan, gazing at the screen.

"Yes."

"It would be difficult, would it not, to equate cancer of the bowel with the idea of a benevolent God?"

"I suppose so. More the work of the devil, I would say."

"Quite," said Brennan. "Ah, there's Thorn."

They watched intently as Kate Reynolds began her interview with Damien Thorn, sitting opposite each other by a coffee table.

"The interview lasts only a couple of minutes," said Harris. "Funny thing. It was a good talk while it lasted. Thorn comes across very strongly. Interesting views."

They watched in silence, Harris leaning forward, sitting on the edge of his chair.

"Any second now," he whispered.

Damien was talking animatedly. The cameras changed, showing the woman listening intently, then caught her glancing to the ceiling, a sudden expression of horror as something crashed past the table. It was the body of a man, suspended, swinging upside down and out of shot.

"There he goes," Harris whispered. "It's not very pretty to watch." He kept up a commentary as Brennan gazed unblinking at the screen. "The poor chap fell from a lighting gantry, caught his foot in a rope, and swung through a set of curtains. The lights exploded and he caught fire."

The screen went blank.

"Wrapped upside down in nylon curtains. The poor bastard cooked to death."

Brennan whistled softly. "Can you run it back to the point where he first appears?"

Harris tapped a button and again the man swung into view.

"Freeze it there."

Brennan moved to the screen and stared at it.

"Run it on again, would you?"

Harris did as he was asked.

"Stop."

Again Brennan peered at the screen, at the face of the man, his face contorted in a scream.

"What do you think that is?" He pointed to a piece of metal in the bottom corner of the screen.

Harris shrugged. "Don't know. Probably a loose bolt from the gantry."

"Not a knife?"

"A knife?" Harris repeated dumbly.

"No knife was found?"

"No."

Brennan took the controls from Harris and silently ran the tape backward and forward.

"They never discovered who he was," Harris continued. "It was a total mystery. But I'm sure there was no knife involved."

Brennan nodded, took out the cassette, and handed it back.

"Well, thank you anyway. Thanks for coming." At the door, Brennan shook his hand. "You won't mention this, will you? Just idle curiosity on my part."

Harris put one finger to his lips and smiled.

"And if there's ever anything I can do for you . . ." said Brennan.

"Well, as it happens, sir, we are planning a series on the social lives of—"

"Quite," said Brennan dismissively. "Talk to my secretary. We'll fix something up."

Harris left the building and called a cab, thinking back to the conversation. Somehow it was disjointed, certainly odd, and he wondered if perhaps Brennan was coming down with something.

Brennan worked conscientiously through the afternoon, waited until his secretary had left, then called home. Margaret was out and he was glad. He did not want to tell her lies. He left a message on the machine that he would be late, back around nine-thirty, then left the office and rode the elevator to the garage.

It took him an hour to clear the early-evening traffic jams and another forty minutes on the minor roads, driving into Berkshire. He stopped twice and checked his map, reached a T-junction, and turned left. It was a narrow country road, flanked with high hedges. A whiff of manure wafted through the window. He closed it and drove on. The road was empty, not even a farmhouse to be seen. He checked his odometer. According to De Carlo's notes, he should be almost there.

Turning a bend, he saw the lights of a pub ahead. He drove into a small yard that served as a parking lot and got out, glanced at the sky. Light cloud cover. There should be a star, he thought flippantly, something to indicate the place of birth.

The lights of the pub were inviting. He looked inside. It was a small place, a traditional ale house, low-ceilinged, with heavy black beams studded with horse brasses. A log fire blazed, despite the warmth of the evening.

He decided he would have a drink first. He could do with one. It seemed these days that he could always do with one.

The publican was a virtual caricature—large with a beer belly, handlebar mustache, red-cheeked, twinkling eyes.

Brennan ordered a large brandy.

"American, sir?"

"No, just a splash of soda."

The publican squeaked with laughter.

"No. I meant you, sir. American?"

"Oh, yes."

Brennan looked around him. Seated around the bar and by the fire was a group of villagers. One winked at him and he smiled back, thinking that any minute now they were going to line up and tell him tall stories for the price of a pint, then snigger behind his back when he left. But it was not like that. The publican had a daughter who lived in Los Angeles and he had visited her the previous winter. Mercifully, Brennan discovered, the man was free of the usual clichés, made a number of reasonable observations, and gave Brennan a drink on the house.

After the third brandy, Brennan felt confident enough to put the question.

"Oh, yes," the publican replied. "Plenty of gypsies around here. Dirty buggers an' all."

"I don't suppose you remember any stories about a strange birth here? About twenty years ago?"

The publican laughed again. "Any gypsy birth is a strange birth, sir, but what did you mean exactly?"

Brennan shrugged. "I'd just heard stories, that's all."

"You a reporter, then, sir?"

"No. Just a tourist."

The publican nodded and moved away to serve another customer. Brennan finished his drink and rose to leave, feeling strangely let down and angry at himself for wasting time, wondering just why he had come and what on earth he had expected to see. He decided that he would have a quick look at the spot and go home to his wife.

He left the pub, saying good night, nodding to the publican and the villagers. They watched him go, then the publican lifted the bar flap, pushed open a half-door, and stood back to let his dog pad out. It followed Brennan across the road, raised its head and sniffed the wind, peered into the clouds, then silently moved forward, its paws leaving no mark in the mud.

He stood on the patch of waste ground and felt cheated. There was nothing but mud and clumps of weed. He felt nothing, not even the hint of reverence he experienced when he entered a church, nothing but the dampness seeping through his soles. He wanted to sneeze and he chuckled, then cursed himself for wasting half an evening.

He turned and could no longer see the pub. Squinting, he moved forward and saw the outline of the roof. They had put out the lights. He checked his watch. Surely they would not close this early? He shrugged. It was none of his business. He trotted back to the car, shivering. A wind had risen and he felt a chill coming on.

Slipping into the car, he was conscious again of the smell of manure, but now it seemed to be on the inside. He started the engine and tapped a button to operate the fan, but it was not working; a red warning light told of an electrical fault. He cursed and hoped that it was just the fan and nothing that would prevent him getting home.

As he drove out of the yard, the first drops of rain splashed on the windshield. The wipers smeared dead insects across the glass. He hit the windshield washers but that too was out of order. The stench was getting worse. Again he hit a button to open a window; again nothing. He cursed and curled his toes in his shoes, feeling the dampness move into his calves.

"Rising damp," he muttered, and grinned to himself. As the car picked up speed, he glanced to his left, thinking that he saw a dog staring at him, but when he was past and checked in his mirror, there was nothing.

He felt dizzy, the brandy clogging his senses, the fumes mingling with the stench of manure. He tried to think back. How many drinks had he had that day? Three. Hardly enough to affect him and certainly not sufficient to make him so dizzy.

The rain was heavy now, clearing the windshield of the insects, but the wipers could barely cope. He peered out. Ahead, he saw the junction. A T-shaped signpost indicated London to the left. The road was empty and he spun the wheel, checked his mirror automatically, and stamped on the brake. Something was hanging from the signpost, something small and pink, nailed to the wood. He reversed and drew closer: nothing, just a trick of the light. Again he blew bad breath and hit the accelerator, but the car would not respond.

He looked to his left and right, spun the wheel again. The hedges raced past the car on either side, as if he was driving fast, but nothing was happening, nothing worked. He had no control over the machine.

He stamped on the clutch and shifted gear, shaking his head again as the dizziness returned. The stench made him nauseous. He coughed and retched, then glanced once more in the mirror. The terrors of his imagination grinned back at him in the shape of the child, laughing at him, toothless and obscene.

Brennan screamed, put his hands over his eyes to banish the sight, and the car slued across the road toward a waterlogged ditch. He was still screaming when his head smashed into the windshield.

Margaret Brennan gazed blankly at the television screen and occasionally glanced at the clock. The phone rang.

"Hi," she said brightly, then shrugged. "No. He's still not back yet. I'll let you know."

She hung up and slumped back on the sofa, her eyes glazing as she continued to watch television. Half an hour later, the phone rang again.

She grabbed it, said "Yes" three times, then "Which hospital? Where exactly?" Then she dropped the receiver and ran for the door.

The child gazed wide-eyed at him, smiled, then winced in pain. He reached out to it, making baby noises, cooing to it, but he could not find its hands. The body was cold and there was a gash in its side. He ran his fingers along the tiny shoulders and felt them pressed hard against a crossbeam of wood, and when he reached the fingers, he found them curled around the head of a nail.

He screamed but there was no sound. He tried to turn away from the sight but he could not close his eyes. In desperation he pulled at the nail, but the baby gripped tighter, and despite its agony, it smiled at him, a smile of pity and forgiveness.

He touched the little pulsing skull and tried to read the inscription scratched into the wood, but it was in Latin and he did not understand.

Surely someone would help. He turned away to run and the stench followed him, the stench of the other child, the one covered with fur and slime, the one with the ever-open mouth and the claws.

He could hear voices now, but he could see nothing.

"Something about a hundred dead babies," said a male voice close to his ear. "Something else about a crucified child."

"Yes," he said, shouting. He wanted to tell the voice, but he could not make himself heard.

"But he's physically okay?" The female voice was anxious. He tried to call her name, but he could not remember it, could not recall the name of his wife. A hand reached for him and he grabbed it; then he felt the jab of a needle and the blackness flowed over him, yet still he continued to cry for help, pleading for someone to come and pry the baby off the cross . . .

The hand was gentle and soft, a female hand on

his brow. He reached for it and caught it, tried to open his eyes, but he could not. He traced the hand with his and stopped at a finger, finding a scab. He heard her voice telling him everything was all right and still he held on to the finger, like a baby, feeling the heat of the scab between his fingers, a cluster of tiny circles. He squeezed harder until he heard a cry of pain, then he felt the jab of a needle again and the blackness converged on him.

When he finally awoke, with his imagination purged, he recognized his own curtains. The throbbing in his temples was painful, but the nightmares had gone. He blinked and tried to remember what had happened, but his memory failed him. He touched his face. There was a bandage around his head. He sat up slowly, felt giddy, and lay back, then swung his legs out of the bed and tried to reach the door, picked up a mirror on the bedside table, and squinted at himself, fearful of what he might see. It was his own face, puffy beneath the bandage, but *his* face.

"Philip!"

He looked up and saw his wife at the door. She smiled, came over to him, kissed him lightly, and swung his legs back onto the bed.

"A fine mess you got yourself into," she said cheerily.

"Tell me."

"You crashed the car. You were found wandering around, covered in blood, and—"

"Did they save the baby?"

"And you've been hallucinating." She smiled as

if to a child. "Not surprising, with that bump on your head."

She stroked his brow and he held her wrist. A fragment of memory danced across his mind and vanished.

"Sleep now," she said, and he half-closed his eyes, then opened them to watch her sway out of the room, rolling her hips like a hooker, and he realized that she had not asked him how he felt. It was as if she did not care. He closed his eyes and sighed, and as he dropped off to sleep, he prayed to God that the baby had been saved.

Chapter 15

For the first time in her life, the ambassador's secretary was lost for words. As she watched her boss pack his overnight bag, she hopped distractedly from foot to foot and run her fingers through her hair.

"But why Rome?" she asked at last. "And why now, of all times?"

"Toothpaste, razor, dental floss," said Brennan.

"You're expected this afternoon at Whitehall. You can't just—"

"Send Harry." Brennan zipped up his bag. "It's only an observation job anyway. Make an excuse. That's what you're good at. I'll be back by lunch tomorrow."

She looked at him, exasperated. "But can't you at least tell me who you're going to see?"

"If I said I had an appointment with a mad monk, would you believe me?" He smiled, and she shrugged back at him. Yes, she thought. The way you've been behaving lately, I'd believe anything.

"See you tomorrow," he said, and left the room,

his bag slung over his shoulder, Band-Aid over his cut forehead, dark glasses hiding a black eye.

She watched him step into the elevator, then stretched out in his seat, spun around, and gazed at the Great Seal, played with the two telephones, stroked the intercom, and ran her fingers along the desktop.

"Pressure," she said aloud. Some of them just can't take it. Far better to be just what I am, she told herself, a foot soldier with no great burden of responsibility.

She got up and patted the chair.

"Just ain't worth it," she said, and sauntered back to her desk.

In the small jet streaking southeast across France, Brennan gently pressed his fingers to the bandage. He could feel the jagged stitches. There would be a slight scar, the doctor had said, but nothing to worry about. He would not be disfigured. It was the scar on the mind that was more difficult to treat.

He drew the telegram from his pocket and read it again. The cablese concealed an emotional plea. The priest was dying and needed to see him. He gazed at the address of the hospital. It should be simple to find it.

He glanced through the window and realized that he was taking a familiar route. Robert Thorn had made this trip, and Doolan, and Finn.

He called to the steward and ordered a drink. "But I'm still warm," he muttered to himself.

"Sir?" The steward looked inquiringly at him.

"Nothing," said Brennan. "Just tempting fate."

The jet landed on one of the outer runways and Brennan was quickly ushered through the formalities and into his hired car. His secretary had phoned ahead and cleared the way for him, and he wondered what the Rome office thought about his request for anonymity: probably nothing. They had enough on their plates without worrying about some diplomat on a private junket.

Driving east, it took him two hours to find the village. The hospital was set back from the road, out of sight. He gazed at the sign and groaned. It had not occurred to him that it would be a mental hospital. He stopped the car by the entrance, leaned back in the seat, and sighed. He had wasted his time. In his imagination he had seen himself standing by a bed talking to a dignified old man who would bless him and expire gracefully. There would be flowers and soft Italian breezes. Instead he was about to encounter some slobbering lunatic.

He spun the wheel angrily, the wheels raising dust as he turned into the drive.

It was a small one-story building with tiny windows. As he walked inside, he felt irrationally afraid. What if they kept him in? No one would find him. No one in London knew where he was. . . . He cursed himself, smiled at the receptionist, asked to see the priest, and gave his name. He was told to wait. A moment later, a young man appeared from one of the corridors. Brennan recognized the face as Brother Francis, and felt a spasm of guilt. If only he had listened to the man before, maybe some lives would have been saved. . . .

"Thank you for your journey." The monk held out his hands, held Brennan by the shoulders, and hugged him. When Brennan stepped back, he saw that the man was in tears.

"How is he?"

"Soon he will be at peace," said Francis. He took Brennan's arm and led him down a corridor.

"Why is he here, though? In a—" The word would not come out.

"An asylum?" It stirred something in his mind, of electrodes and protesting patients. "They said he was making a nuisance of himself, talking about the end of the world, seeking messengers in the village to go to England. We said that we could look after him in the monastery, but they insisted . . ."

Brennan wanted to ask who "they" were, but he followed the monk in silence, feeling, as he always did in hospitals, that those on the inside were different, luckless people. He wanted out immediately, into the air, but the monk, as if reading his thoughts, held him tightly by the arm.

They walked down a flight of stairs into a basement corridor. The air was cooler but the light was bad, as if visitors should not be permitted to see too clearly.

Francis knocked on a door at the end of the corridor. A male nurse wearing a green uniform looked out, nodded, and stepped aside to let them enter. Brennen sniffed carbolic acid.

He followed the monk inside. It was a tiny

room, more of a cell—just a single cot, a washbasin, and a toilet bowl. Instinctively Brennan glanced at the window. There were no bars, but it was too narrow for anyone to squeeze through.

The figure in the cot stirred, raised a hand.

"Mr. Brennan?" The voice was weak, little more than a squeak.

Brennan bent and shook the bony hand. De Carlo's face was almost fleshless, the mouth a dark gash. Brennan shivered as he touched the cold skin. Here was the man who had tried, in his own way, to save the world, this poor madman, and this was his reward, a lonely death in a madhouse.

"Sit down, Mr. Brennan."

He watched the monk reach into the corridor and pull in a chair.

"I am sorry to find you unwell," he said, sitting by the bed.

De Carlo shook his head. "Save your sympathy for those who need it." For a moment the two men gazed at each other in silence.

"You are not a religious man, Mr. Brennan?"

Brennan shook his head.

"Then why are you here?"

Brennan shrugged. "I read your notes and the letters. They made no sense—"

"We are not talking about the rational."

"I cannot believe in devils."

"Then, I repeat, why have you come?"

"Compassion perhaps."

De Carlo shook his head.

"Curiosity, then."

De Carlo smiled at him and Brennan realized

170

that he had indeed made the trip for selfish reasons. He looked at his shoes.

"I think I'm going insane." It was something he could have admitted only to a stranger, and immediately he felt relieved by his confession.

"Look at me," said De Carlo.

Brennan looked up, aware of the absurdity of the situation: he was confessing fears of madness to a man who was himself certified insane.

"Why do you think this?"

Brennan began to describe his nightmares. At first he was flippant, shrugging, smiling ironically, but as he continued, the words poured out of him—about the babies, the child on the cross, the foul-smelling abomination. When he had finished, De Carlo painfully propped himself on an elbow and reached out for Brennan's hand.

"What is the English word for bad dreams, when they become real?"

"Hallucinations," said Brennan.

De Carlo nodded. "The power of evil is unlimited. Distance is no barrier. It can corrupt the imagination. The power of the Antichrist can destroy the minds of men. It has control even over the beasts.

"The force of evil can drive men insane," De Carlo continued. "You recall one of your predecessors. His name was Doyle."

Brennan nodded.

"Damien Thorn needed to get rid of him and so the man was driven insane. He killed himself. No one knew why."

171

"Those whom the gods would destroy, they first make mad," murmured Brennan.

De Carlo shook his head. "Not the gods, my son, not the gods."

The monk was standing by the door. De Carlo looked up and fluttered his hand at him and Brennan was reminded of a dying bird. The monk reached into his cassock and produced a pouch. De Carlo took it and drew out a dagger. "They no longer permit me to keep this," he said. "So Brother Francis must take care of it."

Again Brennan gazed at the figure of Christ on the hilt.

"This is the dagger that destroyed the physical life of Damien Thorn." He paused. "It must be used again."

He handed it to Brennan, holding it by the blade. Brennan took it, the hilt fitting neatly into his palm.

"Hold on to the body of Christ," said De Carlo. He coughed and lay back. "You know what must be done. There is very little time left. The tribes of men are at each other's throats as ever, and soon it shall be over."

He closed his eyes and Brennan leaned close to him to catch his words.

"The Book of Revelation says: 'Woe to the inhabiters of the earth and the sea! For the devil has come down unto you, having great wrath, because he knoweth that he hath but a short time.'"

He opened his eyes and stared at Brennan. "He hath but a short time, Mr. Brennan," he repeated.

172

"Put an end to him. Feel the body of Christ in your hands . . ."

His eyes clouded over and his grip went limp.

Brennan stood up and moved away from the cot. "I do not have your faith, Father," he said. "But I wish you peace."

"That is up to you."

He moved to the door.

"And remember," came the faint voice. "Your nightmares are the work of the devil. But the risen Christ will help. Trust in Him."

Brennan nodded and followed the monk out of the room. The nurse moved forward and closed the door behind them as they walked up the corridor. Brennan heard the old priest cough, a dry brittle sound like a death rattle, and he shivered, glad to be gone.

Driving north, Brennan felt himself curiously at peace. He looked at the dagger that lay on the passenger seat, and the sight of it comforted him. So, he was not insane. His nightmares were the work of some malign force. Things began to fall into place and make some kind of sense to him, and he realized that if they made sense, then maybe he was mad, after all. For who else but a madman would believe . . .? He grinned to himself and gazed into the rearview mirror. His smiling face grinned back at him.

Chapter 16

Like the BBC press officer before him, Kenneth
Evans, assistant commissioner of the Metropolitan
Police, was intrigued by Philip Brennan's invitation to lunch at the embassy, especially as there
was no apparent reason for it. He had met the
man a few times and liked him. He was charming
without being smarmy, and if, like all politicians,
he was devious, then he hid it well—double devious in fact, the policeman thought.

Brennan rose from his desk as he was ushered
in. They shook hands and Brennan apologized for
his appearance.

"Well, sir," said Evans in a tone of mock sever-
ity. "If you will go driving without your seat
belt . . ."

"Quite," said Brennan. "Point taken."

Their lunch was wheeled in and they settled
down to eat. They started talking about the latest
urban riots, then the problems of dealing with political demonstrations, then the Trafalgar Square
disaster, then finally onto Evans' favorite subject,
which was soccer.

After nearly an hour of this, the policeman was

beginning to wonder why he had been invited. It was not until they were drinking coffee that Brennan outlined his request.

Evans frowned. "Five daggers, did you say?"

"Identical. They are in your Black Museum, I believe. It's just that they were found in Chicago some years ago and our museum there would like to exhibit them for a short time. After that, of course, you would have them back."

"I don't know . . ."

"I take it that all the information is on file? Fingerprints or whatever?"

Evans nodded.

"And that they would be required only if a suspect were to be apprehended?"

"That's right."

"Which, without wishing to appear rude"—Brennan smiled—"is not too likely to happen in the next few weeks."

"Correct." Evans returned the smile.

"But if the daggers were required, we would return them immediately."

"I'd have to insist that they were well-protected."

"I'd make sure of that."

"Well, then, I don't see why not . . ."

"Fine. Thank you. Thank you very much. The museum will be delighted."

They went back to talk of soccer and it was another twenty minutes before Evans left, idly wondering what the man wanted with five old daggers.

"Ours not to reason why," he said aloud, breathing out brandy fumes as he climbed into his car. Whatever the reason, the result was that the ambassador would owe him a favor, which was a nice position for an assistant commissioner of the Metropolitan Police to be in. He belched noisily and settled back content.

"Margaret!" Brennan wandered through the house. He knew that she was probably still out shopping, but he needed to make sure. He did not want her coming in and asking questions, because he knew that she would not accept the answers. He poured himself a large brandy and paced the hallway, glancing repeatedly at his watch, aware that he was drinking too much, but the hell with it. He would cut down, once things got back to normal. If they ever did.

"Come on, come on," he muttered to himself. Evans had promised the package would be delivered about six.

The doorbell chimed and he ran to it, pulled it open. A police messenger held out a package to him, asked him to sign for it, saluted, and vaulted onto his motorcycle. Brennan closed the door and went to his study. He scrabbled at the wrapping, cursing as it held firm. It had been well-packed. He picked up a pair of scissors and hacked at it, then tore it apart, pulling with both hands and yelping as one of the blades broke loose and sliced into his palm. He dropped the package and stumbled against the desk, sucking the blood that welled in a thin, precise line.

The daggers lay scattered on the floor, each one

labeled. One had fallen directly on the point and was driven an inch into the parquet flooring, the hilt swaying, its label fluttering like a flag.

As he reached for it, the blood flowed down his fingers and dripped onto the hilt. He swore and ran to the bathroom and pulled out a box of bandages. As he pressed one to his hand, he noticed that the dagger had sliced across the crease that the palmists called the life line, dissecting it at the point where they would place middle age.

He grunted another oath and went back to the study. The dagger still swayed in the floor, the hilt stained with his blood. He pulled it out and wiped it with a tissue, his blood smeared over the body of Christ, staining the face and the torso. Mumbling to himself, he went back to the bathroom and washed it, dried it on a towel, and again returned to the study. He opened his desk drawer and took out the dagger De Carlo had given him, then placed it among the others, arranging them in the shape of a cross.

The six faces of Christ, the features identically twisted in agony, gazed up at him. He stared at them blankly, unable to take his eyes off them. It was like staring into a log fire, gazing at the flickering flames: hypnotic and compulsive.

He did not know how long he stood there, but the sound of the front door opening startled him into action. He gathered the daggers together and shoved them into the drawer, answering his wife's hello and wondering what the hell he was going to do now.

It was the hottest day of the year and humid. The radio disc jockey had announced breathlessly that there was a record pollen count. Buher and the boy strolled in the Pereford garden, the dog listlessly padding behind them. The hum of bees provided a background to the chirrup of crickets while, high above, a lark sang soprano.

The boy sneezed, interrupting Buher's little fantasy about nature's orchestra.

"Bless you," he said flippantly, but the boy did not laugh. He looked tired and ill. No matter how strong the sunlight, he never took on a hint of a tan. He looked more frail in the sun, his cheeks sunken, dark pouches under his eyes.

"Is there any more to be done about the meeting?" he asked.

"Nothing," said Buher. "The ground is well-prepared."

"So. It has come to this. Harvest time."

Buher glanced at him. He was about to ask him what he meant when the boy stopped as if he had been struck. He turned and gazed toward the tree line. Buher followed his gaze. Half a mile away he spotted a glint of reflected sunlight in the woods.

The dog growled softly, the hackles rising.

"He has sent his lackey for me," said the boy. "The agent of the Son of God has come to destroy me."

The dog moved forward, running toward the light, and the boy watched it.

"I feel His presence everywhere," he whispered.

"He permeates my soul. His piety seeps into the marrow of my bones."

Buher shivered. He knew what the boy felt because he had experienced the force of the God Child; each night when he was unprepared, he was conscious of His voice, but in the morning it had gone, leaving half-remembered dreams.

The dog had disappeared into the shrubbery and the boy turned back toward the house. "Pray for me, Paul. Tell the disciples to pray for me. I need all their strength."

Buher watched him go back to the house, walking with the gait of an older man, then he gazed back at the hills. The light still glinted from the tree line. Buher stared at it for a moment, then turned and followed the boy, feeling cold even in the heat of the day.

Brennan let the binoculars hang from their strap around his neck and took a deep breath, sucking the damp air into his lungs. He was trembling. It was the eyes, he thought, dead eyes, expressionless. His feet dangled over the wall and he turned to look back into the woods at the haversack containing five daggers. The sixth lay in his palm. He knew he could not do what the priest had asked. It was absurd. Even to think about it was madness.

He was about to jump back off the wall when the dog came loping out of the bushes toward him. Brennan blinked. He had never seen such a beast, such a concentrated surge of power. Quickly he swunt his legs onto the top of the wall and squatted there, balanced precariously. The dog did not break stride, simply threw itself at the wall, the front paws scrabbling for a hold, the great jaws snapping three feet beneath him.

Brennan stared at it, gazed into the jaws, then into the yellow eyes. The dog backed off, then threw itself at the wall again. It made no sound, leaping at him in silence, the only noise being the clashing of its teeth.

Brennan swayed on the wall, feeling an urge to topple forward, the urge he sometimes got on board ship, staring at the sea, the suicidal desire to dive overboard. He closed his eyes and the image of the child on the cross returned.

He shook his head, trying to force it away, conscious again of a foul odor, the smell of the beast below him. Instinctively he gripped the dagger, feeling the sharp contours of the hilt. He held on to it, gripping it until the crown of thorns pricked his palm. The sudden pain startled him. He opened his eyes and the hallucination had gone.

He drew breath and gazed at the dog. It was motionless now, staring at him, head on one side, looking puzzled.

" 'Thy rod and thy staff they comfort me . . . ' " whispered Brennan as he slithered down the wall onto the far side, and as he picked up the haversack, he heard the dog howl, a long wail of failure.

Chapter 17

Peter Stevenson looked down from his window as the first of the limousines drew up, their passengers lost in a crush of press photographers and television crews. He smiled in satisfaction. So far, so good. Whatever happened from now on, his place in history was assured. He had, almost single-handed, succeeded in bringing about this meeting. The Israelis were to publicly shake hands with the Syrians and Lebanese and in particular with one Lebanese who was the link with the Palestine Liberation Organization. Concessions had been wrung from all sides, and within an hour he would be delivering a historic communiqué.

Just so long as nothing went wrong. He closed his eyes and indulged a fantasy; if only he could have got the PLO to come along, but that was too much to ask. Already he could see the headlines. It would be the most important step toward peace since Sadat made his pilgrimage to Israel, and he prayed that it would be more successful than that poor man's ill-fated trip.

He dreaded to think what would happen if

anything went wrong now. They all had nuclear weapons: the Lebanese, the Syrians, the Libyans, even the Christian Militia. Any one of them in a fit of pique could start the holocaust. But, he asked himself, what could go wrong? The agreement had already been made and what was to happen in the next hour was merely window dressing, for public consumption.

He looked along King Charles Street to Whitehall and saw the Israeli cars arriving. There was a renewed burst of activity among the press men. Crowds of sightseers lined the street, but for once there were no banners. These were mere rubbernecks with no ax to grind. He grinned to himself at his mixed metaphor and made a mental note of it. The crowds were there to watch and tell their children that they had seen politicians go in and out the doors. There was not one CND banner, not one prophet of doom; the protesters had been shattered by the Trafalgar Square tragedy. They were leaderless and in mourning.

He took a deep breath, checked his appearance in the mirror, and made for the stairs. In sixty minutes he would be acclaimed throughout the world as one of the great peacemakers. . . .

For security reasons Philip Brennan drove in a different car from his Secretary of State. He yawned as he glanced at the crowd, aware that some of the cameras were aimed at him and that his molars might well be on the television news that evening. He stepped out and was surrounded.

"Mr. Ambassador, can you comment on rumors

that you are to be recalled on grounds of ill-health?"

"Certainly," he said, pushing through, his aides on either side of him, keeping the pressmen back. "There's no truth in it."

"How are you feeling, sir?"

"In the pink," he said, aware again that he was exposing himself. The comment would go nicely with his yawn. They would have fun with that. . . .

Their cries died away as he pushed through the doors and into the corridor. He followed one of his aides to the conference room and took his seat behind the Secretary of State. The big man turned and acknowledged him with a nod and what seemed to be a frown of concern. He hoped that the secretary did not inquire about the day he was missing from his post, for what would he tell him? How would he justify the trip to Rome?

Still, he thought, there was nothing he could do about it. The meeting began and he concentrated on the interplay of speeches between the contentious factions. The Syrians and Lebanese sat next to each other, the Russians behind them. The OPEC group had been seated together. The Israelis were to the right of the Americans.

As he listened to the speeches and checked them against his agenda, he was conscious that this was his world, the real world, not the world of fantasy, of mad priests and devils.

Peter Stevenson's voice brought him back from his reverie. "The proposition," he was saying, "involves the disputed area of East Jerusalem. May I introduce the Syrian delegate."

A television camera swung to pick up the large Syrian who was tapping his microphone and glancing at his notes. The camera was there to record the signing for posterity, a sole media representative, permitted entry for this special occasion.

The Syrian spoke in his own language and Brennan picked up a set of headphones to listen to the translation. The group listened in silence until the Syrian mentioned the name Arafat, the old man who had survived so many assassination attempts and still clung stubbornly to the reins of power.

At the mention of the legendary PLO leader's name, one of the Israeli delegation got to his feet. It was Simon. Brennan and the rest looked at the little man in surprise as he shouted something in Hebrew.

Stevenson got to his feet, his hands raised like a boxing referee, the color visibly draining from his face.

Without warning, Simon vaulted over the table in front of him and ran across the room. Someone stood up to block him, but he was too late. Simon was carrying something, and when he swung his hand, the light was briefly reflected off it. Brennan blinked. It was a heavy onyx ashtray, swinging in an arc in Simon's hand before slicing into the Syrian's mouth. The man grunted and fell back, his teeth splintering, blood spraying the table. Simon jumped on top of him, screaming at him, and hit him again before he was dragged off.

For a few seconds there was silence, everyone gazing stupidly at the struggle, then there was chaos. The Israelis rushed toward Simon and the Syrians and Lebanese clustered around the injured man. Delegates began to shout at each other and everyone was on his feet, except for Stevenson, who had sat down, shaking his head as if it were he who was hit.

Quietly the Russian delegation gathered papers together and left the room, followed by the U.S. Secretary of State. Brennan followed him, leaving the room in an uproar, the delegates squaring up to one another like pub brawlers. Someone called for order, a high English voice, but there was no order to be had.

By the time Brennan reached his car, the news was already on the radio and by the time he got to his desk, the diplomatic telexes were chattering and the phones were ringing off the wall. It was three hours before he looked up from his desk, his hand numb from gripping the phone.

His secretary looked in. "Your wife asked me to tell you that Mr. Buher's invitation to dinner still stands," she said.

Brennan blinked. He did not know about any invitation from Buher.

"Dinner, sir," the woman explained. "At Pereford. Eight for eight-thirty. She said you'd probably have forgotten."

Brennan thanked her.

"She says to tell you that in view of the present

situation, Mr. Buher has labeled it as the last supper."

"Hilarious," said Brennan, and they smiled mirthlessly at each other.

Chapter 18

Brennan had always been aroused by the sight of his wife making up and dressing for a formal occasion, the sensation equally as strong after six years of marriage as it had been when they were living together. Even now, with all that was going on, he was distracted from the telexes by the movement of her arm as she sat, in a slip, brushing her hair.

He tried to concentrate. The TV news spoke of a storm in an ashtray and reported that the Syrians had sent a letter of protest to the Knesset and that it was thought the Russian ambassador was being recalled from Tel Aviv. That was all they knew. Brennan, reading the diplomatic telexes and the conversations over the security systems, was aware that things were much worse. A Middle East war was now inevitable, and that was the least of the problems.

"What do you think will happen?" Margaret seemed to be reading his mind. She twisted around on the dressing-table stool and looked at him, wide-eyed.

He blinked at her. She had never seemed so desirable. He had the urge to make love to her there and then; maybe, he thought, it was something to do with the possibility of imminent death. Maybe yes, maybe no; maybe it was sheer unadulterated lust.

"It doesn't look good," he said, approaching her. He did not want to tell her what he knew; even half of what he knew would scare her out of her wits. He moved closer but there was no response from her. She turned back to the mirror and picked up a lipstick.

Brennan sighed. "Tell me again," he said. "When did Paul invite us?"

"Last week. I told you. He left a message on the service. I remember telling you about it. You grunted."

Brennan shrugged. He had no recollection of such a thing, but if she said she had told him, then she had told him.

For a moment there was silence, then she turned again. "What's the President doing about this?"

"Screwing it up probably." He could not tell her that he had already gone to the sky, that he was, even now, closeted with his closest advisers in one of the strategic air command posts, and that the plastic cover had been taken off the control console.

"He's not so awful," Margaret said. "He can't be."

"He's a weak man," said Brennan. "A national disaster."

"And it was our host tonight who backed him, wasn't it?" She looked up at him and her voice contained the trace of a sneer. "How can you go to Paul's tonight, darling? How can you justify breaking bread with the paymaster of our national disaster?"

Brennan smiled, bent, and lightly kissed her lips.

"Know thine enemy," he said.

She grunted something and drew away from him, got up from the table, and stepped into her dress, a black Chloe design. As she was dressing, she noticed him fitting a small piece of Bakelite, the size of a domino, into his lapel.

"That bad, huh?"

"Got to keep in touch," he said. "Nearly ready?"

She nodded.

"I'll get the car."

He left the room and ran downstairs, looked back to check that she had not followed him, went into the study, unlocked his desk drawer, and took out the haversack. He could feel the points of the daggers like so many knitting needles. Again he glanced up the stairs before pushing open the front door. He sucked in the damp evening air and coughed. Heavy clouds were building from the east and he sniffed the air like a dog, remembering his father, the old country man who reckoned he could smell rain coming and who told him once that thunder was just God moving the furniture about. There would be plenty furniture moving tonight, Brennan thought grimly.

As he ran across the gravel toward the garage, he did not see his wife look down at him through the blinds.

He started the car and slipped the haversack under the driving seat. The front door slammed and Margaret ran toward the car, adjusting the hem of her dress, her hand over her head catching the first drops of rain.

He leaned across to push the door open for her and saw the strap of the haversack wrapped around the gear stick. He was struggling to push it out of sight when she climbed in.

"What are you scrabbling around at?"

He kissed her on the cheek. "You look terrific," he said.

She thanked him and preened in front of the mirror, checking her makeup for rain damage.

They drove through deserted streets, the cassette player blaring from twin speakers in the back. Margaret sang along with it. He glanced at her. He had been right. She did look terrific, radiant even. He felt like cuddling her, holding her tightly, keeping her face hidden. He wanted to protect her from the world, yet she was the least vulnerable of women. The tape ended and it was time to put the request.

"If I vanish for a while this evening," he said, "could you keep Paul occupied?"

She laughed. "What do you mean? Do you want me to whore for you?" She hooted out the word like an owl, one eyebrow raised quizzically.

"Would I ask such a thing?"

She snuggled into the seat. "Wonder what a seventy-year-old penis looks like?"

"Like a peanut," he said. "Maybe a walnut, on a good day."

She giggled and reached for the tape deck again, and Brennan blew a sigh of relief. She had not asked why he wanted to look around the house. It was as though she was not interested, and it was as well. He did not know what he would have told her.

The motorway exit sign appeared, and as he turned into the slow lane, he glanced at his watch, stopped the tape, and switched on the news.

". . . threat of a Middle East conflict loomed larger when the Russian delegation evacuated its embassy in Tel Aviv. Our political editor, Frank Lyons, says . . ."

Brennan half-listened to what the man said, impressed by the way the reporter gave only so much away so that he might inform but not give cause for panic. He wondered, indeed, just how much the man knew. He touched the piece of Bakelite in his jacket and wondered if he would have time to confront the boy. Again the sight of the dead eyes returned to his imagination. Maybe there would not be time. Maybe the responsibility would be taken from him. He had made up his mind that afternoon what he would do. He would confront the boy and then let De Carlo's God take over. He would guide his hand. If God's will were to be done, then so be it. As far as he, Philip Brennan, was concerned, he would have done his job just by confronting the boy, if boy he was. The rest was up to divine intervention. Whatever he did, it would be the will of De Carlo's God. It would not do as a defense in court, but it would do for him.

"Have you been here before?" Margaret's voice jolted him out of his reverie.

He shook his head. "Why?"

"Just that you seem to know exactly where you're going."

"I checked the map before we came out."

She shrugged and peered through the windshield at the high hedges. A rabbit dashed into a hedge and she grunted.

"Missed the bugger."

He looked at her in astonishment, recalling the young woman he had first known who blushed when she said hell and whose strongest expletive was the word "shoot."

The big gates came into view. He stopped, let down the window, leaned out, and pressed a button in the gatepost, gave his name. The gates swung open and he drove up toward the house.

As it came into view, they could see Buher standing by the open door.

"Peanut," Margaret said, and giggled.

He stopped the car and got out, his toe catching on the strap of the haversack. There was a clink, but Margaret, if she noticed, paid no attention. Buher walked toward them, opened the door for Margaret, and kissed her and welcomed her, then turned to Brennan and shook his hand.

"Good of you to come. I didn't think you'd make it, under the circumstances."

Brennan tapped the bleeper. "I only hope the meal isn't interrupted by this damned thing."

Buher took Margaret's arm and Brennan followed them. He glanced at the sky. They had outrun the thunder, and at Pereford the night was warm and humid, a night to eat good food, drink good wine, enjoy good conversation, then walk in the gardens. It was all so civilized.

He walked into the hallway and nodded a greeting to the elderly butler, then glanced up the curved stairway to the gallery and beyond to the corridor leading deep into the house, narrowing his eyes, wondering where the boy lived. He sniffed, but all he could smell was wood smoke from the log fire in the living room.

Buher guided them toward the French windows, pointing out features of the place, acting for all the world like a tour guide. The butler poured drinks, the logs crackled. Floodlighting illuminated the lawn and the rose garden. His wife looked beautiful, his host was urbane. It occurred to Brennan that the scene could be a commercial for some extravagant product. It could be a commercial for Philip Brennan: successful, happily married, entertained by a rich and powerful man in one of the stateliest homes in England. It was perfection, except for the six daggers nestling in a haversack a few yards away.

"Later I'll show you the gardens," Buher was saying.

"I doubt that you can," said Brennan. "There's a storm on the way."

Buher looked at him and frowned.

"Thunder," Brennan said.

"Ah, yes."

He moved closer as Margaret wandered to the other side of the room, looking at the paintings.

"How bad is it?" Buher asked.

Brennan smiled. "A time to keep your fingers crossed, wouldn't you say?"

"Fingers, toes, anything you've got."

Brennan turned as Margaret called to him. She was standing beneath a portrait. He moved across the room and gazed at the face and the inscription. "Damien Thorn: U.S. Ambassador."

"Told you he was beautiful, didn't I?" she whispered to him, and winked.

Buher joined them and smiled at Margaret. "He was very attractive to women," he said.

"Yet he had no children?" said Brennan.

Margaret looked at him in surprise. "Why do you say that? What's the connection?"

Brennan shrugged and looked at Buher. "I'm surprised that he did not continue the dynasty."

"He was only thirty-two when he died," said Buher.

"Yes. I remember the funeral."

There was an awkward silence, broken by a knock on the door. They turned to see the butler announcing that dinner was served.

Again Buher took Margaret's arm, bowed to her. "I hope you both have an appetite," he said, and led them out of the room.

They crossed the hall to the dining room, the butler showing them to their chairs. A candelabra stood in the center of the table sprouting six black candles. The French windows were open to the lawn. A cluster of stars shone through a break in the clouds.

As they settled themselves, Brennan was tempted to ask why they had been invited and why there was no one else. He knew that Buher normally had some woman as a partner when he gave a dinner party. A politician on a foreign trip would be honored for his wife to act as temporary hostess at Pereford. Yet there was never any hint of scandal.

Tonight, though, the table was set for three, a triangle of cutlery.

He glanced at his wife and again he felt the need for her. It seemed that she had never looked so attractive. It was a weak word, he thought. "Radiant" was better, "ravishing . . ." He shifted in his seat, smiled at her, and watched the butler handing Buher a glass of wine. Buher tasted it and nodded.

"Do you know," Margaret said "when I was a child, I went with my father to dinner at a house in Rhode Island. The host was rich—French, I think—and when his servant brought the wine, he sent it back." She smiled. "He sent back his own wine."

The men smiled and Buher followed Margaret's story with one of his own. Throughout the first course, the conversation was frivolous. The clouds, building up from the east, caused the room to seem even more darkened and in the candlelight Margaret seemed flushed. Brennan watched her surreptitiously, noticing she was drinking more than usual; he wondered why. The night air was becoming increasingly oppressive and he loosened his tie. The candles burned more brightly, without a flicker, six perfect tulip-shaped flames.

A fish course was served, followed by veal. Brennan forced himself to eat, although he had no appetite. He made himself contribute to the conversation, although he had nothing to say. All he wanted was to leave the table and look around the house, to find the boy. As if on cue, the receiver whined in his lapel, silencing Buher in midsentence.

"If you'll excuse me." He got to his feet.

"Take the phone in the drawing room," said Buher.

He nodded his thanks and left the room, glancing back as he closed the door. Margaret and Buher sat motionless and silent, staring at each other.

He had expected the call, but still he hoped it would be nothing, just a false alarm or a routine check, but his palms were clammy as he tapped out the number on the telephone.

"Brennan." It was the only word he said. Twice he grunted, then replaced the receiver. He looked up and saw himself in one of the mirrors. He looked well. He had not gone pale. His heart was not thumping. His pulse was normal. Instinctively he looked through the window at the sky, then turned and walked stiffly back to the dining room and gently opened the door.

Buher and Margaret sat as he had left them. He stood by the table and placed one arm about his wife's shoulders.

"It has begun," he said. "Tel Aviv and Jerusalem have been bombed."

They looked at him but said nothing.

"The satellites have picked it up," he said. "Nuclear warheads. Total destruction. There is no word yet of Beirut, but there will be soon. Any strike on Israel will result in immediate retaliation."

"An eye for an eye," Margaret said. Brennan looked at her. The strap had fallen from her shoulder and her breasts were almost totally naked, but she seemed not to have noticed. Her eyes were bright in the candlelight and he wondered if she was drunk.

He tried to focus his thoughts. If the Middle East was now a caldron, then how soon would the missiles strike elsewhere? He knew the scenario by heart, all the possible war-game plans, but now that it had begun, he could not take it in.

Buher rose to his feet, knocking over a wineglass. The wine dripped like blood onto the floor, but he did nothing.

"The people who have made war against Jerusalem," he said in a monotone. "Their flesh will fall in rottenness."

Margaret pushed back her chair and stood next to him, gazing at him.

"Their eyes will rot in their sockets," she said. "Their tongues will rot in their mouths."

Brennan called her name and reached for her, but she ignored him.

"There shall be a great shaking in the land of Israel," said Buher.

"So that the fishes of the sea and the fowls of the heaven, and the beasts of the field, and all creeping things that crawl upon the earth . . ." she continued.

". . . and all the men that are on the face of the earth," said Buher in the same tone, "shall shake at my presence, and the mountains shall be thrown down, and the steep places shall fall, and every wall shall fall to the ground."

"Margaret!" Brennan touched her arm and drew back. The flesh was hot, as if she were in a fever. He shook his head, recognizing the words they spoke, remembering them from his Bible classes. He could recall them vaguely but he had no idea that she was so well-versed. And still they continued:

". . . every man's sword shall be against his brother," they said in chorus. "And I will plead against him with pestilence and with blood; and I will rain upon him and upon his bands, and upon the many people that are with him, an overflowing rain, and great hailstones, fire, and brimstone."

Margaret laughed, a high cackle, and Brennan backed away from her. As he reached the door, he saw them hold hands and her words came back to him: "Do you want me to whore for you?"

"And when ye shall see Jerusalem compassed

with armies, then know that the desolation thereof is nigh," said Buher.

Brennan thought back to the young monk. It all seemed so long ago, in another age, when there was still some hope.

"For these be the days of vengeance," said Margaret, "that all things which are written shall be fulfilled."

As he backed away down the hallway, he could still hear them:

"And Jerusalem shall be trodden down of the Gentiles, until the times of the Gentiles be fulfilled . . ."

He stumbled to the door, no longer sure what he was doing, knowing only that he must find the daggers and find the boy before he could leave this place.

He pulled open the car door and dragged out the haversack, swung it over his shoulder, and grunted as the daggers pierced his jacket and scratched his back.

He thought back to the old priest's words: "The risen Christ will help you." He repeated them. It was now up to Him. It was His responsibility. He would find the boy and let the hand of De Carlo's God guide him.

As he reached the stairs, he looked up into the face of the dog. It stared down at him, then turned and padded soundlessly along the corridor as if guiding him. He ran up the stairs and followed it, single-minded now, thinking only that he must find the boy.

The corridor was dark. At the end, a black door stood ajar. The dog pressed against the wall, allowing him to pass. He pushed the door open and blinked at the sight before him, and in that instant he knew that everything he had been told was true.

The boy was dressed in a black cassock and knelt by the corpse, his lips moving in silent prayer. Brennan took two steps inside, the daggers clanked inside the haversack, but the boy did not turn. It was as if he were hypnotized.

Brennan moved silently toward the effigy of Christ, gazed at it, and saw the dagger in the spine. It was all true. His skepticism had been a false guide. He stared into the eyes and turned to look at the corpse, shivering at the sight.

Briefly he closed his eyes and prayed for guidance. When he looked up again, he knew what he must do but was not convinced that he had the strength. He wanted desperately to leave the place, to take Margaret's hand and run from here, drive anywhere, but the agonized face of Christ held his gaze as if He were alive.

He stepped around to the back and pulled out the dagger. It slid easily from the wood, and he held it loosely, the candlelight flickering off the blade. Words from his childhood came to mind, strange little songs he had learned at his mother's knee, children's sayings he thought he had long forgotten. Again he looked into the face of Christ and wondered why he had been chosen, one who had long ago ceased to be a believer. He touched the face, someone's idea of a Messiah, but not his idea; still, it did not matter. He touched the crown of thorns, thick nails driven into the skull, then laid the haversack on the floor and drew out the six daggers.

The boy still knelt by the feet of the corpse; Brennan grasped the hilt of the dagger he had pulled from the cross, held it in both hands.

"The first extinguishes physical life," he murmured. The boy's back was slim, and through the cassock Brennan could make out the knobs of the spine. And he knew he could not do it this way. He would need to turn him, even if it meant gazing into those sad dead eyes.

"Forgive me," he murmured, reached out, and grabbed the boy's shoulder, twisting so that he turned.

The boy looked up at him, white-faced, his eyes glinting yellow, and smiled.

Brennan drew back the dagger, forced himself to stare into the eyes, sucked in breath . . .

The door flew open and a shaft of light illuminated the room. In the instant he was hit, he smelled the foul breath, grunted as he was smashed to the floor by the force of the impact, the dagger slithering from his grasp, the dog going for his throat. He reached for the massive head, thumbs gouging at the eyes, his elbows pressing into its chest, then turned and held on to the lower jaw with one hand.

The dog shook its head and the teeth dug into his hand. He yelled out, a roar of pain, as the beast pinned him to the floor, shaking its head, its saliva dribbling into his face and running unchecked into his mouth. He choked, then spat into the yellow eyes and briefly its grip relaxed, enough for him to roll and to reach for the dagger with his free hand. He scrabbled for it as the jaws clamped together again on his hand, the dog pinning him again, then unexpectedly switching the attack, biting into his shoulder, the great head twisting, trying to break his neck as if he were no more than a rabbit. Brennan grunted in pain, feeling something snap, the arm beneath him turning numb. He twisted and stabbed upward, slashing at air.

Again he swung the dagger and felt it connect, the blade scraping through fur and gristle. The dog howled and fell away from him. He brought his knees up to his chin and rolled, spinning against the foot of the cross, out from under the weight of the animal, then he looked up as it came for him again, the jaws snapping at his throat, and this time the saliva was flecked with blood.

For an instant he felt sympathy for the wounded animal, an insane desire to take the great head and comfort it. Instead, he drove the dagger at its throat, closing his eyes as he struck home, the force of the blow dislodging the dagger from his grasp, and then there was blackness as the dog collapsed on to him, a splintering sound, and a thud as the cross toppled over and smashed. The dog was whimpering and Brennan could feel its blood on his face.

He kicked out and rolled to one side. The face of Christ stared at him, the body cracked along the spine from the fall. He tried to struggle to his feet as the boy slowly moved toward him, smiling down at him. Again he kicked out and the dog moved, the dagger lodged in its shoulder. In that instant of pity, Brennan had missed the throat. He dragged himself free and lay back against the cross, looking up at the boy, and now he knew why he had been brought here, why Buher had invited him. They had wanted to get rid of him. They had wanted a final confrontation. They wanted the daggers so that the creature in front of him would finally be out of danger.

Painfully he dragged himself to his knees. His right arm was useless and hung limply by his side. He tried to move the fingers, but there was nothing. He could feel blood at his neck flowing down his back and he had a desperate desire to sleep, just to close his eyes and drift away from this abominable place.

The boy gazed down at him, then turned as something blocked the light from the corridor. Brennan twisted and saw Margaret standing framed in the doorway. Her body, in silhouette, appeared to be naked.

He grunted at her as she moved toward him, held out his good hand so that she could help him to his feet, but she turned away from him toward the boy. Brennan blinked and shook his head. He was hallucinating again and De Carlo's words once again came back to him.

"He has the power over the imagination . . ."

The sight before him must be a hallucination, like the child on the cross, the sight of his wife caressing the abomination and going down on her knees before it.

He closed his eyes and felt a scream build in his throat. When he looked up again, he did not believe that she was gently drawing the dagger from the shoulder of the beast, did not believe that she was holding it in both hands as she came toward him, still did not believe that she was smiling at him as she drew back the blade.

He shook his head and raised his arm too late as the blade came closer, and he still did not believe the pain and the shock. He opened his mouth as he toppled onto his back, his eyes fixed on the hilt as it swayed gently, did not believe that the blade was buried in his neck, that the blood that pumped from his jugular was *his* blood, and that his last sight on earth was the Christ on the hilt gazing down at him, the face reflecting his own agony.

She pushed herself away from the convulsing body and looked down at her dress, which was soaked in his blood. And still the blood pumped from the artery even as he died, spraying the chapel, drenching the broken Christ figure on the cross.

The boy held out his hand to her and led her to the embalmed corpse.

"Kneel," he said, and she did as she was bid. Looking up, she saw the candlelight flicker in the eyes and it seemed as if he was smiling at her, as if he was alive and blessing her for what she had done.

"His spirit is alive in me," said the boy, reading her thoughts. "And now is the time of destruction."

"Amen," she whispered.

She turned, to see the dog struggle to its feet, lick the wounded shoulder, and limp toward her. It looked from one to the other, then licked the hands of the corpse, smearing the fingers with its blood.

The boy reached out and drew Margaret to her feet.

"Seek his strength," he said.

She held the body, her arms tight around it, and heard the boy kneel by the toppled cross, turned, and saw him gaze into the face of the Christ.

"So, Nazarene," he sneered. "You are defeated. You, who demanded of mankind that they eat of your flesh and drink of your blood, where are you now?"

He pointed to Margaret.

"Look," he said. "Is this the creature you hung on the cross to save? Is this the creature made in the image of your Father. Look at it! Soiled with the blood of her husband, she lusts after *my* father. Was it worth the suffering, Nazarene?"

He grasped the crown of thorns and gazed into the face.

"The world is in its death agonies and the

whore sits upon the beast. The prophecies are about to be fulfilled. Soon it will be over."

He got to his feet and smiled, and the chapel was silent except for the soft murmuring of the woman and the whimpering of the dog.

Chapter 19

Paul Buher drained his glass and gazed into the night sky, imagining that he could detect a glow from the east. Soon there would be no need to use his imagination. The scenario had been written long ago. It needed only the right players and the right sequence of events. Mankind had chosen destruction, the only irony being that it was a common ashtray that had acted as the tinderbox.

He left the table and wandered into the drawing room. The fire had gone out. He switched on the radio and poured another drink.

". . . confirmed reports that Jersualem, Tel Aviv, and Beirut have suffered nuclear attacks. From Washington, the White House and the Pentagon are denying that the President has left the city and has taken to the air. Our Moscow correspondent has been unable to file his report and indeed all lines from the Warsaw Pact countries are dead. The Prime Minister is due to make a statement shortly and it is understood that the ambassadors from all NATO countries are due to arrive at Number Ten Downing Street within the hour . . ."

He snapped the radio off and sighed, feeling his age. He was an old man and it was time to die.

"Three score and ten," he muttered, then turned and wandered slowly out of the room. The butler stood in the hall and they looked at each other. Both men shrugged their shoulders as if there was nothing more to be said. Buher clutched the banister and hauled himself up the stairs, then padded down the corridor toward the chapel, wondering where the woman had gone.

Long before he reached the door, he could hear the whimpering of the dog. The door was open, but at first, with the light behind him, he could not make out the details. For a long time he stood leaning against the frame while his eyes adjusted to the gloom, and even when he saw, he could not believe. The chapel floor was awash with the blood of Philip Brennan. The boy and the woman knelt by the body of Thorn, muttering something indistinguishable.

Slowly he moved forward, gazed down at Brennan, at his incredulous expression. He touched the hilt of the dagger, wiped his hand on his trousers, then forced himself to draw it out, but he had no strength and he needed to put his foot on the chest before he could remove the blade.

That done, he gathered the other knives together and looked down at the boy.

"He came to destroy me, Paul. And perished."

Buher nodded, hoisting the haversack over his shoulder. "I will dispose of these once and for all," he said.

But the boy paid him no attention.

Buher stared into Brennan's face. Such an innocent, he thought, but brave. They had tried to
drive him mad but they had failed, and so they
had to entice him into a trap. He touched the daggers and turned, tapped Margaret on the
shoulder. She looked up at him, her lips moist,
her eyes opaque, and he was reminded of the days
before he needed to buy whores, when women
looked at him like that. The blood was still wet
on her body. He reached down and pulled the
dress up over her breasts, but she smiled at him
and drew it down again, pouting at him, then licking her lips and leering up at him, her body
reminding him of the night not so long ago when
she had grasped his hand and the mark of the
beast had been transferred to her finger.

He remembered the time she had been recruit-
ed two years earlier, a classic case, initiated, like
so many others, through sex. She had been invited
to Pereford one weekend when Brennan was out
of the country; he remembered reading the report
from the other disciples, how she had at first
resisted and protested, but when she had given in
to the temptation, she had become the most enthusiastic of them all, and when she had been
finally let into the secret, she had been ecstatic.

The diabolical conversion of Margaret Brennan, the report said, was one of the most
successful ever made. He looked at her and shook
his head. Human beings were so predictable, so
malleable.

She reached out for him, but he brushed her

hand away and tried to ignore her whispered obscenities.

As he backed away, he remembered a photograph of her in the file. A picture of her as a beautiful child with a radiant innocent face, her head cocked inquisitively like a puppy—innocent and yearning for knowledge, a knowledge that she had soon found.

He moved past her, stepped over the dog, which lay panting, looking up at him with clouded eyes, and knelt behind the embalmed body. A delicate steel frame supported it. He began to unscrew the clamps that were fixed to the buttocks and held the body upright.

"Paul?" The boy looked inquiringly at him.

"His last request," said Buher. "At the moment of Armageddon. The final mockery."

The boy frowned. "I never knew . . ."

"He wanted to stand on the ground of his enemy at the final moment, to denounce Him."

Still the boy looked doubtful.

"Take the cross and follow me." Buher's tone was commanding and the boy nodded.

Buher unscrewed the final clamp and the body fell back into his arms. It was not heavy, but he had little strength and stumbled back against the wall. Margaret ran to help him and together they dragged the body out of the chapel.

At the door they stopped and Buher glanced back. The boy had lifted the cross and was carrying it over his shoulder, his knees buckling under the weight, while the dog heaved itself to its feet and followed them, limping, the blood seeping from its wounds.

Slowly they made their way along the corridor and down the staircase, the feet of the corpse bumping on the stairs and leaving a trail of powdery skin.

Behind them, the boy held on to the banister and struggled with the cross. Halfway down, it slipped, and he shrieked as the crown of thorns stabbed him in the neck and shoulders. He cursed and pried it off, then continued, but now he too was bleeding, thin trickles running down his back and staining the cassock.

The thunderclouds were heavy and the first drops of rain spattered them as they came out into the driveway. The tiny ruined church, built with the house, stood on a rise behind the shrubbery, two hundred yards from the west wing. Buher remembered hearing that Damien, as a boy, had wanted it to be demolished, but he had been persuaded to let it stand as a reminder of the waning power of Christianity. Later, as a young man, he had forced himself to enter the church, conquering his fear, so that by the time he reached maturity, he could tread easily on the hallowed soil and gain strength from the desecration.

But the boy had never attempted to enter. He had not his father's strength. He would not go within fifty yards of the place.

As they struggled up the hill, nothing else moved, not a bird nor an insect. The hedgerows were still, as if every living thing was watching and waiting.

As they came closer, the boy shouted for them to stop, but Buher kept going. Margaret was panting, the sweat trickling down her body making tracks in the bloodstains. She mumbled incoherently and occasionally smiled lecherously at Buher. He ignored her and pulled the corpse up the hill, feeling his heart batter against his ribs and his breath rasp in his throat.

"Paul!" the boy roared at him. Buher stopped by the church gate and propped the corpse against the gatepost.

The boy struggled up to them with the cross.

"Place it there," said Buher, pointing to a spot by the wall. "So that they can be together, the victor and the vanquished."

Again the boy did as he was told, then stepped back, touching the puncture marks in his neck from the nails, his eyes wide with fear as he gazed at the church.

"It was your father's wish," said Buher again. He looked to the east and he could see the sweep of the hills against the sodium lights of the main road and the paler lights of the village.

"It is time," said Buher, watching the boy back away from the church and go down on his knees.

"Go to him," he whispered to Margaret. "Give him your strength. Pray with him."

He watched as they knelt together twenty yards away, their heads bowed. The dog limped across to them and lay in the grass. He took a deep breath, clasped his arms around the corpse, and dragged it through the gate, the feet bumping against pebbles, past the old wooden church sign which read:

THE PARISH CHURCH OF ST. JOHN

He stumbled and the corpse pitched onto its face. As he picked it up, he heard the boy scream his name and saw him run toward the gate.

Breathing heavily, he dragged his burden to the door, praying that it would not be locked. He propped it against the wall and pushed. The door creaked on its hinges. He glanced back and saw the boy at the gate, motionless, fear holding him back.

Buher dragged the corpse inside and pushed the door shut.

"Please," he whispered to no one as he searched in the darkness for the bolt. He found it, tried to move it, but it had rusted.

"Please, God," he muttered, thumping the bolt until his hand bled. Slowly it slid into place as he heard the boy run up the path, heard him roar, felt him throw his full weight at the door, the impact sending the corpse tumbling to the ground.

Buher reached for it and dragged it by the heels along the nave. The pews had long since rotted away, leaving only the stone altar and pulpit.

"Buher!" The boy's scream echoed through the building as the head of the corpse scraped along the floor, leaving a trail of torn skin.

He could hear the boy run around the building, scrabbling like a rat at the walls. Reaching the altar, he clasped his arms around the chest of the corpse, heaved it upright, and let it drop, the skull smashing against stone.

He turned it over, onto its back. The face had been crushed in the fall and was unrecognizable. He stretched it out on the altar, slipped the haversack off his shoulder, and scattered the daggers on the ground.

"Buher." The boy's voice was pleading now. He looked up and saw his fingertips at the top of the wall. Buher reached for the first dagger and looked down at the corpse on the altar.

"You promised control, Damien, but you delivered destruction. You were a false prophet."

He raised the dagger in both hands and brought it down, his eyes tightly closed. The skin cracked with a sound like a gunshot, and from the wall the boy screamed. Buher stumbled back, retching at the stench of escaping gas. He scrabbled in the dirt for the second dagger and forced himself to look again at the corpse. Foul-smelling gas hissed from the wound, causing the police label on the hilt of the dagger to flutter.

Forcing himself to keep his eyes open, he drove in the second dagger, then the third, and the fourth . . . As each blade pierced Damien's body, the boy screamed, his voice changing in pitch until it became the howl of a jackal.

Finally, one dagger remained. Buher looked at the figure of Christ on the hilt and crossed himself. He thought back to the beginning of his conversion, some young man whose name he had forgotten talking about three score and ten years; then there was the pity he had felt for the old nurse, the horror when he saw the pictures of the dead girl, then the creeping realization that his life had been a betrayal.

He raised the dagger and drove it into the stomach of the corpse. Damien Thorn sighed, a last gasp of air hissing from the open mouth as Buher slumped to his knees, gazing along the two lines of daggers, planted in the shape of the cross. He closed his eyes and heard a long sigh of despair, and when he opened them, the body had disintegrated, the daggers scattered among a pile of bleached bones. Buher got to his feet and again he made the sign of the cross over the skeleton with the skull and jawbone of a jackal.

He turned away and moved slowly to the door, unbolted it, and stepped outside. The boy was on his knees and Buher stared at him. He was a pitiful sight. There was no spirit left in him. He looked at Buher with dead eyes, then crawled away from him. Beside him the dog lay dead.

Buher made his way up the path to the woman, who stood by the gate, looking down at her hands in horror, trying to wipe away the blood, as if she had just awakened from a dream.

"Cover your nakedness, woman," he said softly.

She looked at him as if he were a stranger, then pulled her dress up over her breasts.

"It is done," Buher said.

Together they walked toward the house. The sky had cleared and was bright with starlight. Armageddon was over, and the world had survived.

And I saw an angel come down from heaven, having the key of the bottomless pit and a great chain in his hand. And he laid hold on the dragon, that old serpent, which is the Devil, and Satan, and bound him a thousand years, and cast him into the bottomless pit, and shut him up, and set a seal upon him, that he should deceive the nations no more, till the thousand years should be fulfilled: and after that he must be loosed a little season.

REVELATION 20:1–3.

Recommended Reading from SIGNET

	(0451)
☐ CUJO by Stephen King.	(117298—$3.95)*
☐ FIRESTARTER by Stephen King.	(099648—$3.95)
☐ CARRIE by Stephen King.	(111494—$2.75)
☐ THE DEAD ZONE by Stephen King.	(093380—$3.50)
☐ NIGHT SHIFT by Stephen King.	(099311—$3.50)
☐ SALEM'S LOT by Stephen King.	(098277—$3.50)
☐ THE SHINING by Stephen King.	(113349—$3.50)
☐ THE STAND by Stephen King.	(098285—$3.95)
☐ ONE FLEW OVER THE CUCKOO'S NEST by Ken Kesey.	
	(088670—$2.25)
☐ SAVAGE RANSOM by David Lippincott.	(087496—$2.25)*
☐ SALT MINE by David Lippincott.	(091582—$2.25)*
☐ THE TRIBE by Bari Wood.	(111044—$3.50)
☐ TWINS by Bari Wood and Jack Geasland.	(098862—$3.50)
☐ THE KILLING GIFT by Bari Wood.	(098854—$3.50)
☐ BRAIN by Robin Cook.	(112601—$3.95)
☐ SPHINX by Robin Cook.	(097459—$2.95)*
☐ COMA by Robin Cook.	(097564—$2.75)

*Prices slightly higher in Canada

Buy them at your local
bookstore or use coupon
on next page for ordering.

Sensational SIGNET Bestsellers

(0451)

- [ ] **BRAIN by Robin Cook.** (112601—$3.95)
- [ ] **THE DELTA DECISION by Wibur Smith.** (113357—$3.50)
- [ ] **CENTURY by Fred Mustard Stewart.** (114078—$3.95)
- [ ] **ORIGINAL SINS by Lisa Alther.** (114485—$3.95)
- [ ] **MAURA'S DREAM by Joel Gross.** (112628—$3.50)
- [ ] **THE DONORS by Leslie Alan Horvitz and H. Harris Gerhard, M.D.** (113381—$2.95)
- [ ] **SMALL WORLD by Tabitha King.** (114086—$3.50)
- [ ] **THE KISSING GATE by Pamela Haines.** (114493—$3.50)
- [ ] **THE CROOKED CROSS by Barth Jules Sussman.** (112032—$2.95)
- [ ] **CITY KID by Mary MacCracken.** (113365—$2.95)
- [ ] **CHARLIE'S DAUGHTER by Susan Child.** (114094—$2.50)
- [ ] **JUDGMENT DAY by Nick Sharman.** (114507—$2.95)
- [ ] **THE DISTANT SHORE by Susannah James.** (112644—$2.95)
- [ ] **FORGED IN BLOOD (Americans at War #2) by Robert Leckie.** (113373—$2.95)
- [ ] **TECUMSEH by Paul Lederer.** (114108—$2.95)
- [ ] **THE JASMINE VEIL by Gimone Hall.** (114515—$2.95)*

*Prices Slightly Higher in Canada
